Really?

Susan Hahn

Contents

Dedication

I dedicate this book to my husband, Ted. Without him, this book would not exist!

Acknowledgments

I'd like to acknowledge Kate Bedel and Gary Woodruff who encouraged me to write a book. Without their constant support and encouragement, I would not have tried.

About the Author

Susan grew up in a farming community and still lives there with her husband of over 50 years. They have 1 son and 1 daughter. Besides writing, she always enjoyed cooking and baking which led to making wedding cakes, cupcakes and cookies for the last 48 years. She also plays the piano, organ, saxophone and is now learning how to play to Mountain Dulcimer.

The Demon Pressure Washer

Ted and I have hosted a Fourth of July party every year for the last twenty years. It has grown bigger and bigger as the guest lists grew until we ended up with over 150 people this year. I love entertaining, so all the work it takes to get to it is well worth it to me. Besides, having a party forces me to get everything done by the deadline. Otherwise, I may put stuff off that I shouldn't.

May was a very wet month this year, and I didn't get a chance to get started on my projects until June. That gave me one month to spruce up the yard, the house, and the garage. Hard work never killed anyone, I don't think, but I'd better have the tools to do my work with, and they all better be in working order, or I'm not a very pleasant person to be around.

I decided to start out by power washing our patio and pool area first. I dragged the power washer out, got everything hooked up, and started washing the deck around our pool. There was not much pressure, but it was taking the winter grime off the white panels. Suddenly, the power washer died. Really? It had plenty of gas and oil, so why did it just die? I pulled and pulled on the starter rope, and it finally started up again. It worked for a few minutes, then died again. Sigh. Again, I get it started, thinking it just needed to get woken up from its winter nap. I was trying to be patient and kind.

Started. Stopped. Started. Stopped. By now, my blood pressure had risen, and I was really getting angry. I am not a very patient person, and when I get in the cleaning groove, I do not want to be bogged down with equipment that does not work! Again, it started, then stopped. Okay. I guess I thought if I screamed at it, it would suddenly realize that I was serious and it better start working and stay working. Nope, it was as stubborn as I was and died again after just a few minutes. By then, I figured out that not only was it not staying on, but when it was working, it was only about half the pressure it should have been. Heck, I could spit harder than that thing was spraying. I nudged it with my foot. All right…I kicked it, screamed at it, kicked it again, and it would not start at all. My daughter, who lives across a pasture field, heard the screaming and came rushing over, thinking I got seriously injured, one of our cats got wounded, or I was yelling at Ted again.

I'm standing in a puddle of sweat, glaring at this stupid machine, when oblivious Ted comes around the corner to see how I am getting along. He says he did not hear me yelling and swearing, but I think he just waited until he had backup before he approached ground zero. "What is the matter? Are you alright? It cannot be that bad." Yes, yes, it can be that bad because I had a list of things I needed to accomplish that day, and it was not going to get done with that demon washer! I was almost in tears because I was so frustrated. I told Ted to take the stupid washer to the dump and buy me a new one! He agreed, which was the healthiest decision he made in a long time.

As it turns out, there was a new business that sold all kinds of yard equipment that just started next to his office, and he went there the next day. He called me on the phone and said the owner had two different types of washers. There was a small one, and there was a bigger one. Ted said it was my decision as to which one we bought. Always go big or go home, right?

"Get the big one! That way, I can reach my second-story windows and clean the siding way at the top without a ladder!" He hates it when I climb ladders, so I knew that was a good selling point. He brought the big one home, unloaded it, hooked up the hoses, gassed it, and proceeded to start it. Man, did that thing have power! I was so excited I felt like Tim, the Tool Man, Taylor! After supper, we would go back out, and he would show me the steps to starting it. There were a couple more steps than our old one, but I could handle that.

The next morning, I could barely wait to get Ted out the door so I could start power washing everything that did not move. I followed Ted's instructions to the letter, reached down, and pulled the starter rope and "Snap," there was such a huge recoil when I pulled it; the rope almost broke my wrist! OUCH! Well, that wasn't supposed to happen! I tried it again with the same result! I had to wait until Ted got home that night so he could see what I was doing wrong. I was so bummed—no cleaning for me today.

That evening, Ted got home and figured out what the problem was! He was always so good at figuring stuff out. He said this monster had so much pressure built up that we needed to figure out a way to keep the water flowing through it while I was trying to start it. That would release the pressure so there would not be such a recoil. But it was impossible for me to hold the trigger with one hand and pull with the other. I said just to take the darn thing back to the store and get the smaller one.

The next day, he went back to the store, explained the situation to the owner, and said he would be more than happy to take it back, but Ted would have to pay a restocking fee of $200.00. If no one knows Ted, I will just say that he is "frugal." Ted would risk his life in the middle of a six-lane New York interstate to pick up a nickel, so I knew a broken wrist was not going to make him cough up $200.00. He would figure out a way that I could start it.

The following evening, he came up with a brilliant plan! What we need to do is use a zip tie and tie the trigger open, releasing the pressure, and it would free up both my hands to pull the rope. Then, I could cut the tie off and start power washing. That made sense!

"Here…I'll show you," he says rather smugly! He zip-tied the trigger open, laid the hose with the trigger attached to the ground, and yanked the starter rope. Ba-ROOM! It started with one pull, sounding like the cars at the 500! Then, in a split second, the hose with the trigger started flying in the air like a bucking bronco, zigging and zagging, diving and lurching! It turned itself around and headed straight for us! The stream of water shooting out could take the skin off a cat! The nozzle whacked me in the leg, and blood started gushing. Then, it turned and hit Buckley, our nosy German Shepherd! Not content with putting a gash on my leg, it turned again, and the powerful stream of water hit my toe and almost cut it off! Blood gushed again!

I started screaming, "Step on the hose! Step on the hose!" as I limped away. After jumping out of the way a few times, Ted finally stomped on the hose and bent down to grab the water-spraying nozzle. He held it like they do in all those documentaries on TV about catching rattlesnakes in the wild west. They hold the snake by its neck, and the rest of its body is wiggling every which way to get loose! He finally managed to shut that deadly water weapon off, and the hose went limp. REALLY? By now, I'm glaring at him, trying to stop the blood flow, and tell him very softly, "Take that damn thing back!"

I bandage myself up and go back outside. I am pulling weeds in the flower bed when Ted comes outside about an hour later. "I think I know what WE did wrong!"

"What WE did wrong? We? I had nothing to do with this debacle! Don't you mean What YOU did wrong?" I showed him two big bandages on my leg and toe. "Yeah, whatever. We, I mean I, should not have left the nozzle in the trigger! It is still too much pressure. We need to leave the nozzles out until we get it started. Look, I will show you!" I took several steps backward, out of the hose's reach, while he removed the nozzle and started the machine! The hose just lay on the asphalt, spraying out water and doing no harm. Then, all I had to do was cut off the zip tie, put in the nozzle I wanted to use, and power wash to my heart's content! Okay, I think it might work. I had to write down all the steps it took before I could start the machine, but I was able to start it with one pull, all by myself! So, I will not sign the divorce papers yet.

I bought an attachment for the old power washer a couple of years ago. It was a big round covered brush that sprayed water and spun at the same time, scrubbing all the dirt away in one big swath. It would cut down on the time it took me to wash my asphalt driveway and concrete walks. It just never worked like the advertisement showed with our old washer, but now I know it was the washer itself. It just did not have enough power. I hooked it up to our new washer and anticipated the cleaner leaving a bright shiny patch on my driveway. But instead, up into the air, it flew! There was such a powerful stream of water coming out from underneath the scrubber it launched my scrubber into the sky like the space shuttle! It went about eight feet up, then just hung there. I managed to pull the hose and the attachment down and shut off the washer. I needed something to weigh it down. I saw two large, lonely bricks in Ted's garage, so I zip-tied them on top of the scrubber, and Bingo! They were heavy enough to keep the scrubber on the ground. My driveway looks great, and I got it done in the tenth of the time it usually takes me. Finally, a happy ending!

Sprucin' Up The Garage

Early this spring, I was visiting a dear friend of mine. She had just gotten her garage floor done. She had hired a gentleman to paint and epoxy her floor, and it was stunning. I was jealous! Her floor was beautiful, gray with little speckles in it. I wanted one just like it in my garage! We have two garages…one is "mine" that is attached to the house, where I park my van. The other one is "Ted's," where he parks his truck and yard equipment. My garage floor was anything but pretty. It had grease stains, paint stains, and any other stain you could possibly think of on it. We entertain during the summer, and we usually set up the food table in my garage. It occurred to me that the floor could be the cause of appetite loss. (My daughter said that is carrying it a bit far, but it made for a good argument.) Since my friend and I are close, I had no qualms about asking her if the floor was awfully expensive. The figure she threw at me almost made me not want it. Almost.

I went home and started researching. It turns out the average Joe can do it themselves! Hum…a light bulb came on! I pulled up YouTube (don't you just love YouTube?), and sure enough, there was a lady showing how she did her garage. A lady! No burly, muscular men, but a lady! If she can do it, I certainly can! I looked up the epoxy she used, and several home improvement stores carried a kit that contained everything I would need. How easy could that be? It was not that expensive either.

The next step was convincing Ted to let me do it. I fixed one of his favorite meals, and when his tummy was full, I approached him with the idea. "Hey!" I said. "Look at this," as I showed him the YouTube video. "Isn't this neat?" He nodded a very small yes. "Can I do this? Please?"

"Let me think about it," he said discouragingly. (I know his mannerisms.) Over the next couple of days, I badgered him until he consented. I guess he knew it was fruitless to argue with me because I was going to do it regardless of his opinion. This was for his own good. Who knows what kind of germs were lurking on that floor? He has some health issues, so if I covered them, I could save his life! What a great argument! He cannot deny a life-saving procedure!

He gave in, and off we went to the nearest city to the home improvement store. We found the floor kits. Now we have to decide what color we want. My vote was tan, so we got tan. They had different-sized kits, and the salesperson and Ted decided we needed the one-car garage kit.

I said, "Are you sure? Don't you think we need the 'two and a half car' garage size?" I could see it in their eyes...stupid woman, even after I explained that I was planning to do the inside of the closets also.

"No, you'll have more than enough," the salesman said. Okay. Who am I to argue with a man? (Do not answer that.)

I took their advice as "experts." Now, we needed to wait for the perfect weather conditions. It is a simple process, but it has many steps, and it takes at least a week to complete. I needed warm days without rain, and our weather was cool and rainy. Finally, the meteorologist said what I wanted to hear! Lots of sun all week and no precipitation! Perfect! I was so excited. I started unloading the contents of my garage and closets over to Ted's garage. I even moved a refrigerator, a chest freezer, and a stove by myself! Geez! Where did all that stuff come from? I started pitching stuff along with piling up the "keep" items in Ted's garage until we could not get in the doors! He will have to park outside for a few days. I think that might have slipped through the cracks when we were discussing the maneuver. At the end of the day, my garage was completely empty, and I was ready to start the first step.

I was up bright and early, got Ted out the door for the day, and was ready to tackle the first step, which was power washing the floor. I prayed I could start the thing! I do not want to have to wait for Ted to come home. I got the washer hooked up, gassed up, zip-tied the handle open, took the nozzle out, and all the rest of the steps it took for me to start it. My adrenaline must have been high because I closed my eyes, and with one gigantic pull, it started roaring! Hallelujah! I power-washed the floor, poured cleaner on it, scrubbed it, and power-washed it again. I re-read the instructions, and yep, it said I had to let it dry for twelve hours. I gathered up all our fans and pointed them in all directions to give the floor a higher chance of drying faster.

The following morning, I hit the floor running. On to step 2. Etching the concrete. That was an easy step to do. Just mop it on, rinse it off, then wait another twelve hours until the floor is dry…again. The next day, the floor was ready for the water barrier. Our garage floor was always damp after rain, so this was a must. I applied the moisture barrier, then rinsed, and again waited for the floor to dry. This is getting old, but I was determined to do it right.

Finally, the last step is the preparation for paint. I have been good so far and followed the directions to a "T." Usually, I am a bit impatient with these sorts of things, but I can hang on for one more day. I patched the cracks in the old concrete and let it dry overnight. Is anyone counting? This is day five already, and I have not even begun to paint!

Today is the day! It is Friday and I am gung-ho! I get to paint! I love seeing the results of all my hard labor. The paint comes in a silver Mylar-type bag with a seam down the middle. The paint is on one side, the Epoxy is on the other. They are not to be mixed until you're ready to use it. I popped the seam and squished the bag, mixing the two together. After it was mixed, I poured it into an ice cream bucket. I slowly poured a small spot on the floor, and I could not believe how well it covered! Next, I get to sprinkle these tiny, colored chips over the wet paint. I love it! I continued on until I had about half the floor done. My bucket was empty! I only had half enough! I knew I should have gotten a second kit! The instructions say to do the entire floor at one time, so there aren't any transition lines. I was livid! My blood was boiling! No one in town carried the kits, so I was going to have to go back to the big store! Grrr…!

I ran upstairs and quickly threw on a respectable pair of shorts and a top, ignoring the big paint splash on my leg. I drove like crazy, ran into the store, scanned the shelf, and grabbed the very last one in tan that they had. Boy, was I lucky. I drove back home, changed clothes, mixed the paint in the bag, and poured it into my bucket. That is strange…it does not look the same. I took a swipe with my paint roller, and it was clearly a different color! REALLY? Both boxes said tan. Why doesn't it match? Words do not describe how angry I was. I checked the store's competitor since I had taken the last box off the first store's shelf. Yes! They have the kit in tan, but I also noticed there were other colors available, one being Mocha. That is what this wrong color is! Mocha! Stuck in a box marked Tan!

I changed clothes, my legs still covered with paint splotches, grabbed a stir stick covered with the first paint, put a lid on the bucket, and flew to the first store. I marched to the service desk, put the bucket on the counter, and told them I wanted to return this paint. "Oh, honey. We can't take that back."

I grabbed my stir stick, opened the lid on the bucket, and said, "Do these two colors look alike to you?"

"Are they supposed to be?"

"YES, they are both supposed to be tan. One of these is clearly not tan!" The girl looked at the painted stick and the paint in the bucket. When she looked back up at me, she said she'd get her manager. I have been told that once in a great while, my eyes will flash what I am thinking, and today must have been one of those days.

The manager came over, looked at the paint bucket, then looked at me and said, "Go ahead and refund her money." I told them thank you and told them I knew it was not their fault. I was just frustrated because I only had half the garage floor done. I took my money, ran to the van, and pointed it in the direction of the other home improvement store. I ran in and found the box I was looking for. Yep! It is identical to the one I have at home (but then again, so was the wrong one). I double-checked the color; yes, it said TAN. I [paid for it, I ran back to the van, and headed home as fast as my vehicle could take me. I am not sure if you noticed or not, but I did a lot of running that day! As a rule, I do not run anywhere, but this day was different. I literally ran! People probably thought I was nuts! "Look at that old lady with paint all over her legs running like someone is chasing her!"

When I got home, I mixed the paint up and held my breath as I cut open the bag and poured it into my bucket. It looked pretty close! I poured some on the floor and rolled it next to the original paint. It was a tiny bit lighter. Maybe it will get darker when it dries. I had no choice but to keep painting the floor, regardless of whether it was a perfect match or not. When it started drying, it did not get much darker at all, and I noticed that it did not have the glossiness that the original paint did. Oh well. I am over this stupid project. Besides, there is always going to be something parked over the transition line, so no one will probably notice except me. I will notice it every single day, and it will drive me crazy.

Ted came home from work, looked at the paint job that I was still working on, and just shrugged. I asked him why he was so pessimistic, and he said, "I just don't want to see you get heartbroken when our van tears all this paint up."

"Really? The paint is made for cars to drive on!"

Then he says, "Did you lock the cats up?"

We have three rescue cats that live upstairs in our garage. It is their kitty condominium. They pay their rent by keeping the mouse population down. It is carpeted, warm in the winter, tolerable in the summer, and out of reach from our German Shepherd, Buckley. He would love to get ahold of them, but the big coward is scared of stairs and will not go up to the kitty condo. The cats know this, so they taunt him by looking over the edge of their condominium at him, and then they strut back and forth, tails high in the air, waving slowly back and forth like they are thumbing their nose at him. It drives Buckley crazy, and I swear I can hear the cats snicker.

Ted asked me if I locked the cats up in the cage upstairs. "Nope. They haven't come down all day, and I know they won't until the paint is dry."

"Well, I think you'd better lock them up."

"Oh, for gosh sake! Fine! I'll lock them up!" I put down the paint roller and stomped upstairs. I grabbed the cats and threw them into this large cage we have; only one slipped out before I could get the door closed. No big deal. He will not cause any trouble. I went back to my painting. I was almost done! I was getting close to the door that goes into the house. Suddenly, I heard the most horrible, ear-piercing, nails-on-a-chalkboard screech. The two cats that were in the cage could never get along, and they were in a knock-down-drag-out fight! Then, it came. Big puffs of black fur, just snowing down onto my wet paint. I could not reach it because it was beyond my arms' length. I could not walk on it and repaint it because I was scraping the bottom of the bucket as it was, and I still had a little more floor left to do. All I could do was stand there and look. Tears were welling up in my eyes; murder was in my heart, but I wasn't sure who to kill first…the cats or Ted for suggesting the idea.

The next morning, I went downstairs and opened the door to the garage. No, it wasn't a nightmare. There was my brand-new floor with wisps of black fur, standing straight up, with just the bottom glued into the paint. The paint was dry, so I did the only thing I could do. I found an old straight razor and proceeded to shave my floor! The little black splotches on the floor at least took my mind off the fact the paint wasn't exactly the same. Unfortunately, they are in a place that cannot be covered up, so every time I go in and out, I see them. My only pleasure in this whole job is to hear Ted say that maybe the floor will not peel and fall apart after all.

A vacation! Really?

Why does the word VACATION stir up so much excitement and anxiety at the same time? I try to be an optimist, but in reality, I know something weird is going to happen. It always does. Not your typical flat tire, getting lost, or delayed flight. Those are for amateurs. I'm talking about things like having the engine fall off your airplane, getting mugged in a foreign country, flying with an expired driver's license, or having a bear climb all over your brand-new car. But the very worst vacation that comes to mind is the "Trip from Hell," as we like to call it.

As I was packing for this three-day business and pleasure trip, I was dreaming of a "Cleaver" vacation. (You know…Ward, June, Wally, and the Beaver) I'd wear pearls all day long, and we would go frolicking on the beach during the day and dance and eat lobster by candlelight. Not together, though. We have a hard enough time trying to dance without a lit candle and buttery fingers.

Bright and early, we headed to the airport. We have a connecting flight leaving Chicago for Cancun. Once at the airport, we get ready to check-in, and they need to see my driver's license. Being a tad bit OCD, I usually have all my paperwork in clear page protectors neatly arranged in a small binder and tucked into the outer pocket of my carry-on. This time, I forgot to stick my driver's license in the folder and left it in my billfold. No biggie. My purse is highly organized as well, so I can find my driver's license without even looking. (Sometimes, I even amaze myself!)

We get the "All-Clear" from security and check our boarding passes to see where our departure gate is. The ticket said F34. REALLY? We walked past gate A1 and took a tram to gates C, D, and E. We had to get off at E because that was all the farther it went. We will be hoofing it the rest of the way to "F." We walk, and we walk, and we walk. At one point, I checked to make sure we had not crossed the state line. Finally! There was "F." "F1, that is. F34 was the last gate at the end of that terminal, so we walked some more. When we got there, we plopped down in the first seats we saw. There was hardly anyone sitting in that section, which I thought was odd, but I was too tired to care. The time to board came, and no one said a thing. Ted overheard a couple of gentlemen talking behind us about going to London. Wait! What? We went to the counter and asked the flight attendant when we would be boarding the airplane to Cancun since our flight was supposed to take off in ten minutes!

She said, "Oh, didn't you get the text? Your flight has been moved to Gate E13." No, I did not get a text! We reached Gate E13 at record speed only to be met by an attendant who said our flight had just taken off. She was going to make us pay for new tickets since the ones we had were non-refundable, but she must have looked at two Hoosier Hicks and saw how desperate and tired we looked and took pity on us. She put us on a much later flight and did not charge us any extra. Thank you, lady, whoever you are!

We are finally in the air, headed to Cancun to an all-inclusive resort for some R and R. Nothing can go wrong now. We enjoyed an uneventful flight and finally landed. We got off the plane, and I reached for my binder to get my passport ready for customs. My passport was gone! Ted's passport was there, but mine was not! I know I had brought it because they needed to see it in Chicago! I tore my organized purse apart and my carry-on. No passport. It dropped out on the plane. I started back down the runway to check my seat on the plane when I was met by a huge, burly man who told me I was not allowed to go back on the plane. I explained the situation, and he said he would have the flight attendant look for it.

We waited half an hour, but they could not find it. Now I'm starting to really panic! As Ted and I sat there, trying to figure out what we were going to do, I glanced down at my carry-on. Hmmm…. Why does it look weird? I opened it up for at least the fifth time but could not see what was making it bulge out. Then I saw it! A small tear in the top of my lining inside the carry-on. I could barely get my hand into the hole, but I did, and there was my passport! When I stuck it back inside the bag, I must have slipped it into that tear. Thank you, God!

We got through customs, collected our luggage, and caught a shuttle bus to our resort. It took us about an hour to get there, but I did not care at this point. I was drained, physically and emotionally. I needed some sand, sun, and surf.

Our room was very nice! There was a balcony that overlooked the ocean and lots of space to spread out. We dropped our bags, and I told Ted I was going down to the gift shop to get some sunscreen. When I went to pay the clerk, I realized my billfold was missing! I went into a major panic mood! I had most of the money and credit cards in my billfold. I ran back to the room and started tearing through everything. I was sick to my stomach. Someone stole my billfold! I started crying, and when Ted walked in and I told him what happened, I think he wanted to cry, too. I got on the phone and was dialing Life Lock to cancel all my credit cards when my phone call was interrupted by someone calling me.

It was a gentleman from our airport back home who said I had left my billfold on the counter when I got my driver's license out. "Thank you, thank you," I said. He told me he was going to personally lock it up in their safe, and when we come home, I can ask for it. What a relief!

"Let's go get something to eat," Ted said. "I'm starved, and they say they have a great seafood restaurant out by the pool." That sounded wonderful, so off we went to fill our tummies and celebrate the fact that we actually made it here and my billfold was found.

The restaurant had a seafood buffet set up that night. All kinds of exotic dishes, with some tame dishes thrown in. I was not very sure that the seafood and buffet went together, along with ninety degrees and high humidity. Surely, the Board of Health would make sure their cooking facilities were up to standards. Ted was being quite adventurous and had put a little bit of everything on his plate. He wolfed it down and went back for seconds. All done with our meal, we went for a walk along the beach, only we did not make it to the beach. We made it to the first restroom we found, where Ted proceeded to get violently ill. I got him to our room, got out my first aid kit that I always take on trips, and fished out a couple of Pepto Bismols for him to take. Then I tucked him in for the night and figured he would be better by morning. Boy, was I wrong! He was in the bathroom more than he was in bed, and I swear his face was green. (He reminded me of Shrek, but I did not tell him that).

The next morning, he was still extremely sick, so I went to the front desk and asked for the resort doctor. He came to the door in just a few minutes and gave Ted a good going-over. He told us what I already knew…food poisoning, an unbelievably bad case of food poisoning. I had a tough time understanding what he said since he was a native of Cancun, but I figured out he wanted Ted to go to the hospital. That was not going to happen! I heard too many horror stories about Mexican Hospitals. "No. Let's just let him stay here. I will stay with him, and if he gets worse, I will call you." The doctor reluctantly agreed and gave Ted a shot for the severe nausea and some pills to help with everything else. He told me to get him some Gatorade and make sure he keeps drinking it.

I went to the reservation desk downstairs and asked them if they had Gatorade. Nope! No Gatorade anywhere at the resort. I would have to go into town and find a grocery store. So off I went, on foot, out the back door of the hotel, looking for a grocery store. I finally spotted one. A tiny, sleazy-looking hut with three men sitting on the doorstep, smoking cigarettes and staring at me as I walked up. I excused myself and walked past them into the store, found a couple of bottles of Gatorade, wiped the dust off, and went to the cashier. All I had was a $10.00 bill, and I handed it to him. I have no idea how much Mexican money I needed, but the clerk got a big smile on his face, took my $10.00, put my Gatorade in a bag, and shooed me away like a fly. Where is my change? Surely, I had change coming back. But I figured the odds were stacked against me with four men glaring at me, so out the door, I went and headed back to our room. Ted was still sick, but he was finally sleeping. I am not sure what knocked him out…the shot or the pills…but at least he was resting. I spent the day in the room with him, just sitting on the balcony, watching the waves hit the shore and texting my friends.

That evening was the awards ceremony and dinner for the company we were representing. Ted really wanted to go, so he forced himself to get dressed, and we went down to the banquet room. The smell of appetizers and dinner drifted throughout the room, and I could see him turning into Shrek again, with his face turning that same shade of green. He was a trooper, though, and said he was going to stay. Dinner was a lovely filet mignon loaded with mashed potatoes and some sort of weird vegetable that I was not going to touch. I have never seen Ted turn down a good steak, but he did that night. He suffered through the boring awards ceremony, and then we swiftly headed back to our room. I gave him another pill, and he was able to sleep. I sat on the balcony, listened to the waves hit the shore, and texted my friends again.

The next morning was the last full day we had at the resort. The following day, we were going home. Ted still felt kind of off, but he said he might be able to keep some toast down. At noon, he seemed to be feeling a little better and continuously apologized for ruining our trip. I did not care. I just wanted him to be well. He said he thought he felt good enough to go down to the beach and sit in a lounge chair. We found two empty chairs, and I dragged them under a palm tree in the shade. It was a lovely afternoon, just enjoying the sunshine and the water. Then, out of the clear blue sky, a huge seagull came swooping down, aiming right at me, and relieved himself on my head!

Back to the room, we went to get cleaned up and find some bland food for Ted. Trying to find bland food in Mexico is almost impossible, but I managed to rustle up a couple pieces of bread and some fresh fruit. Ted went back to bed, and I packed for the trip home. By now, I could not wait to get out of this place and get home. What a nightmare it had been!

During the night, Ted woke me up with loud moans. I jumped up and asked him what was wrong. He said his legs were hurting, so I pulled the covers back and saw that his legs were as red as a Santa's hat! He got a severe sunburn on his legs, even sitting in the shade! How did he get so burned?

I soaked bath towels in cold water and laid them on his legs, rotating them all night to give him some relief. But I was still puzzled about how he got this burned. The writing on the pill box the doctor gave us was in Spanish. I should have taken Spanish in high school, but the counselor talked me into taking Latin! (That was a useful class if you ever wanted to know about Cyclops.) I could not read any directions, so the doctor transcribed it in English, and I wrote it down on a piece of paper. Later, I had someone tell me what the box said. It said: Warning: Do not stay in the sun while taking this medication. It may cause severe sunburn. Well, that would have been nice to know ahead of time!

In the morning, Ted put on a pair of jeans and walked like he had two boards up his pants legs. He hurt so bad. As we sat down in our seats on the plane, I said, "Thank God we're going home so we can be done with this nightmare!"

The plane landed in Chicago, and we went through customs and then on to security. I always go through first because Ted always gets held up in the metal detector with his titanium hips. I collected our belongings and watched as Ted was getting the wand, the pat-down, and all the other stuff they did. I needed to see when our connecting flight home was departing. I looked up at the big screen, followed it across to our destination, and just burst out laughing. I almost doubled over laughing so hard. Everyone was staring at me when Ted came over and asked me what was so funny. All I could do was laugh and point. "Look!" He looked at the board and saw that our connecting flight had been canceled due to ice and snow!

The authorities at the airport said we had two choices. We could stay at the boarding gate and try to sleep in the chairs, or we could go down into the belly of the airport and sleep on a cot in a dark hallway they do not use anymore. We chose the cots. There were about twenty of them. These tiny little cots were lined up side by side down this corridor. There was a blanket and a pillow on every cot, but who knows if they had ever been washed. Ugh. As tired as we were, though, we decided to make the best of an unpleasant situation and lay down with all our belongings safely tucked between us. I had no trouble fitting on the cot, but Ted, being six foot tall, hung off both ends and sides of the cot. About then, an elderly gentleman, about 113 years old, came down the hall and announced he was the guard. He assured us that we were safe to sleep because he was going to keep watch over us all night. Well, okay. That made me feel a little less uneasy until I noticed he was sound asleep in his chair.

It was a long, long night, and I looked and smelled like a junkyard dog.

I had no hairbrush, no toothbrush, no makeup, wearing yesterday's underwear, and I did not even care at that point.

Our plane was ready. It had been de-iced and ready to roll. An hour later, we were at our home airport. Now, all I had to do was go to the airline ticket counter and grab my billfold, and we would be in our van headed for home. I walk up to the young man behind the counter and tell him who I am and why I was there. The guy looked at me like I had monkeys flying out of my ears. Apparently, he did not get the memo. He told us we should check lost and found downstairs because they have a safe. We took the escalator down to the Lost and Found department. Does anyone besides me remember Rocky and Bullwinkle? The flying squirrel and the moose? There were two villains on the show named Boris and Natasha. I found out where Boris and Natasha went after they lost their jobs on the show. They started working at the Lost and Found! Oh, my goodness! This man and woman were the spitting images of the villains, and they even had a Russian accent! I explained what I was looking for, and they had absolutely no recollection of any billfold being turned in. I asked them to check their safe, and they said there was no need because they knew there was not a billfold in it. We went back upstairs and reported what Boris told us. The young man just shook his head and muttered something under his breath about somebody being a jerk.

Anyway, back to the missing billfold. The young man was nice and said he was going to call the gentleman who first discovered the billfold, and he would find out just what he did with it. Yep! My billfold was in the safe in their office! However, no one had access to it besides him and another guy who was also gone.

"Dang it," he said. If I can come back on Monday evening, he works until 9:00 p.m., and he will have my billfold for me then. So, we headed home.

We finally arrived home, and I wanted to jump out and kiss the ground, but I was afraid I would not be able to get back up. I wanted a shower, a toothbrush, a comb, and my own bed.

We licked our wounds all day Sunday, and by Monday, we were halfway back to ourselves again. We headed to the airport, which is about an hour's drive from our house after

Ted got off work. We were traveling down the interstate, knowing we had plenty of time to get there before the guy left. Then, in the twilight of the evening, we start seeing red taillights. Lots of them, and they were not moving! Traffic was backed up for miles because a car and a semi-truck got tangled up, and the driver of the car got killed. So, we sat there, watching the time tick away. Then, for some reason, traffic started moving ever so slowly and then stopped again. However, it moved forward just enough that we could take the exit ramp. Ted said he knew a shortcut to the airport. Oh dear. That is never good when he says he knows a shortcut. If anyone has ever ridden with Ted, he loves to take shortcuts, which usually turns into "twice-as-long-cuts." But I was desperate and let him do his thing.

We arrived at the airport at about 8:45 p.m. and ran up to the counter just in time to catch the guy as he was putting on his coat to leave. He explained that he had to move my billfold, along with some other items, down to Lost and Found for some weird reason, so down the escalator, we went again! There was Boris and Natasha! Geez! Don't they ever go home? The supervisor told them to get the billfold. They told him we would have to describe it first! I told them exactly what it looked like and how much money it had in it. Out comes the billfold, and they begrudgingly handed it to me.

Natasha even said, "There it is. It still has $535.00 in it." How did they know it had $535.00 in it? Yes, it did have $535.00 in it, but it now had different denominations of bills than what I had put in it originally! I knew Boris and Natasha were villains! I suspected they were counting on me not coming back for it, and then they would have some extra money to buy squirrel and moose bombs! As we rode the escalator back upstairs, the supervisor just shook his head and whispered something under his breath about someone being a jerks.

A Relaxing (Really?) Lake

Adventure!

Ted and I had not been anywhere for a year, so when our friends invited us to go to Dale Hollow Lake in Tennessee for a few days, we jumped at the chance. It would be a very laid-back vacation, just the four of us relaxing on a tri-toon boat during the day and eating at seafood restaurants in the evening. (A Tri-toon boat is just like a Pontoon boat, but with three "toons," instead of two, for extra stability.) We were going to be staying at a magnificent house built on the edge of a mountain. This home had every luxury you could imagine, from a hot tub overseeing a breathtaking view to a beautiful cobblestone courtyard with a firepit and overstuffed couches. There were wrap-around porches with fireplaces to take the nip out of the cool, night mountain air and refrigerators to keep your beverages cold for the warm, sunny days. Every window and porch gave you the high mountain view of the lake below. The inside was even more spectacular, featuring three gorgeously decorated floors. It had enough bedrooms to sleep thirteen people comfortably, even though there were just the four of us, plenty of bathrooms, two full-size kitchens, and games galore just in case the weather kept you inside. It was going to be a paradise for the next few days.

We have two different vehicles. Ted has the small pickup truck that he uses for work, and I have this super full-size van that we bought so I could deliver wedding cakes and haul kids and grandkids. It is extremely comfortable to take on long trips since it has lots of head and leg room, a TV, and the back seat lays down to become a bed. It is also super tall, so I can stand up in it without bending over. It also means I cannot take it in an automatic car wash or most parking garages. But 99 percent of the time, it is just me running to town for groceries and errands, so the TV, the extra head and leg room, and the bed are useless. But it is nice to know they are there if I need them. I am only five feet tall, so I get a lot of strange looks when I climb down out of this oversized chariot. I just recently had a lady come up to me in the grocery store who said her husband, and she could not believe it when someone as short as me could drive that big rig. (I didn't want to burst her bubble by telling her I drove tractors and pulled seventy-foot grain augers down the interstate!)

On the rare occasion that Ted drove the van, it was a ten-minute ordeal for him to adjust the seat back far enough and low enough so he fit behind the steering wheel and see out of the windshield. Then he had to mess with the side and rearview mirrors and got them so far out of whack that I only saw the sky. Anytime I must drive his truck, I always try to leave his settings where they are, but it forces me to sit on the very edge of the seat so I can reach the pedals with my tiptoes, and if I want to see in the rearview mirror, I must stand up. So, we usually just stick with our own vehicles. Another reason I really do not care for Ted to drive the van is that he tends to fall asleep! He says he does not get sleepy driving the pickup, but the van puts him out like a light. Sleeping and driving usually do not mix, so I prefer to do the driving. But whenever we went somewhere together, he would give it the old college try.

The conversation used to go like this:

Ted: I'll drive.

Me: No, because you always fall asleep when you drive.

Ted: I promise. I won't fall asleep.

Me: I've heard that before.

Ted: No, really. I'll be fine. You just sit back and enjoy the trip.

Me: sigh. I know how this is going to end.

Ted, fifty miles down the road: Would you mind driving? I can't keep my eyes open.

Me: I knew it! I knew it!

So now we do not have that conversation anymore. I climb behind the wheel, and Ted jumps in the passenger side, and off we go. About twenty miles down the road, Ted is sleeping like a baby, and it's just me, SiriusXM, and my GPS.

This trip was a pretty easy drive since it was mostly interstate. Then came the drive to get to this mountainside house. Holy Moley, was it wicked! I've seen cow paths more friendly than this road. It was only wide enough for one small vehicle, so the tree branches were rubbing both sides and the top of the van. The house was only approachable from the top of the mountain. There was no way on earth that my van could drive up that road because it was so steep and curvy. Plus, they must have had a downpour because there were gullies carved out on the roadsides where the water eroded the rocks and dirt. I went about four miles an hour, and that was much too fast, but I needed the momentum to climb up the mountainside! We finally found the driveway, and I was able to get the van maneuvered in after spinning my tires and throwing a few rocks over the edge of the mountain. Our friends drove their four-wheel-drive crew-cab pickup truck, and they barely made it, so I was feeling pretty smug with myself!

The next morning, we checked the weather forecasts. Clear skies, warm and sunny all day! It was going to be a perfect day on the water! We rented one of the new tritoon boats and loaded it with snacks, coolers filled with drinks, life jackets, and towels. We had sunscreen, sunglasses, maps, and our phones for calls and pictures. We thought of everything! Off we went to explore this 28,000-acre lake!

It is very easy to get lost on a lake like this. Every cove looks the same, and there are twists and turns that can get you going the wrong way very quickly. But we had a pro at the wheel, and between the map and the GPS on his phone, he navigated us to a great marina to eat lunch, then back on the water we went to head back to our marina. All of a sudden, the winds picked up, the sky turned black, and the lightning became vicious! An aluminum boat wasn't the greatest place to be, with lightning and thunder all around! Then the rain came. Buckets and buckets of rain! To our left, we saw a man in a kayak trying to row his way to shore. He was rowing into the wind, so he wasn't making much progress at all. We decided we'd better go rescue him. We idled up to him and asked him if he needed help.

"No, I'm fine," was his reply. Frankly, he did not look fine, so we asked again. "Well, okay. Just throw me that rope, and you can pull me." Ted told him to tie up his boat and climb aboard our craft. "No. I'll just hold the rope." This can't possibly end well, but we did what he wanted us to do. We started for shore very, very slowly, with the man and kayak in tow. Within a blink of an eye, the kayak flipped, dumping him and the entire contents of his boat into the water. He managed to save one thing. A CPAP machine! What the heck was he doing out on the water with a CPAP machine? For all of you who don't know, a CPAP is an air machine that people with sleep apnea use at night to force their airways to stay open. But in a kayak? We grabbed the box from him, and he begrudgingly climbed aboard. My, we caught us a biggin', as Al Bundy would say! I was shocked he could even fit in the kayak. All four of us got the opinion that he was a college-educated idiot, trying to tell us what to do and talking to us very condescendingly like we were two-year-olds.

Mr. Personality, he was not! He went on to explain that his girlfriend (I was shocked he had a human girlfriend! I figured she was a blow-up doll) and he camped on a small island overnight and that she already left. He tried to tell us her kayak was faster than his! Isn't the speed of the kayak controlled by how fast the passenger rows? At any rate, he filled us with a bunch of know-it-all malarkey and continued to tell us the best way to tie up his boat, the best way to do this, the best way to do that. He was good at talking but not so much at helping the guys out physically. We girls tried to stay out of the way, so we stood back and watched all this play out. The rain was coming down harder than ever, and our guys were soaked to the skin. Ted was bent over the back of our boat, holding the rope tight to keep the kayak from drifting off. Mr. Know-It-All bent over, and his pants came down just as Ted turned to look at him! All Ted saw was a huge moon that was staring at him inches from his face! Fortunately, my friend had her phone and took several priceless pictures that will work to our advantage if we ever need to blackmail Ted!

We finally made it to shore and got Mr. Know-It-All unloaded with all his belongings. He was so entitled that he didn't bother to thank us for helping him. In fact, I bet he told his girlfriend that he had it all under control until we forced him on our boat. As his girlfriend did all the work carrying his belongings to shore as he supervised, I checked her out for any air valves because no human would ever date this arrogant, entitled, know-it-all! If you're reading this, Bozo, it would be to your advantage to take a few lessons in etiquette, gratitude, and humility! Some people might have become cynical about helping others after an interaction like we just had, but we all agreed that if someone needed help, we would certainly help. Also, I think 99 percent of people who need help show real gratefulness when they're helped out of a sticky situation. Besides, when I help someone, no matter how big or small the good deed is, I feel better about myself.

The rain stopped, the sky became bright blue, and the sun came out again. After this adventure, though, we were ready to head to the marina and call it a day. Needless to say, Mr. Know-It-All was the subject of our conversation for the rest of the evening!

The next morning, all four of us were ready to climb aboard the boat and explore the other end of the lake. About midmorning, we ventured into a cove and decided to cool off by taking a dip in the water. Ted is not a fan of water since he cannot swim, so we bought him a sixty-foot rope to tie onto the boat, and then he would have a lifeline to hold in his hand. Since he was wearing the life jacket and had ahold of the rope, he was feeling pretty safe. My friend, who is also leery of the water, does this exact thing when she goes to the lake with her grandkids. It gives her the courage she needs to join in the fun and still feel she is safe! I thought it was a great idea, and it really worked! Time passed quickly as we were enjoying the water until we realized we were all starving and we needed to eat lunch. We climbed aboard and found a marina that had an excellent restaurant. We had a delicious meal and then headed back out to explore another cove.

We found a nice, secluded cove and climbed down into the water. About a half hour after we were there, I noticed something in the water on the other side of our friend. At first, I thought it was just a small tree branch, but as it got closer, I realized it was alive! It was a snake! The way it held its head out of the water resembled a cobra, ready to strike! It turned to look at our friend, then it looked at me, then back at him. When it looked back at me again, it decided to chase me! What the heck! I am not a fast swimmer. In fact, I would not call what I did swimming!

When I was about eight years old, my mother joined forces with five other mothers in the country neighborhood, and all the kids got signed up for swimming lessons at the YMCA. I do believe it was done not for the children's water safety as much as for the carpooling. Each mother only had to drive the ten miles to town once a week! I was the youngest and the smallest in the group, and the people in charge of the swimming lessons would not believe me when I told them I was in the same grade as the rest of them. So, they stuck me in the little kid group, which was humiliating. I have never liked getting my head underwater. I figured I must have drowned in a previous life. My instructor, Miss Hitler (Adolph's niece, twice removed), was determined to break me of the fear. How? Well, let me tell you.

She grabbed my head, forced it underwater, and held it there until I thought I was going to pass out. That did not break me of my fear; it only made it worse. So, while all my friends were promoted to the deep end of the pool, where they could dive off the diving board, I was still in the minnow class with all the rest of the little kids. When the awards ceremony came, all the parents were there, clapping and praising their children for diving and swimming, and I was at the shallow end, just standing, not getting my head wet. I know I was a huge disappointment to my parents. To this day, I do my own interpretation of swimming. It may be ugly to watch, but I can get where I need to go, and my head does not get wet.

On this particular afternoon, I took that swimstyle to the next level! I never swam so fast in all my life! Whenever I looked behind me, the snake was getting closer. I finally made it to shore, but my life jacket was so heavy I could barely move. I didn't want to take my eyes off of the snake, so I did a crab walk up the steep, shale-covered bank. I was afraid that the snake was going to come right up on the shore and get me, so I shucked my life jacket off, and then I was able to stand up and get to higher ground. Everyone was yelling at me to wait until they brought my shoes to me because I had to walk on the shale rock, and they were afraid I'd cut my feet. Once I had my shoes, I walked with them in my hand. I wanted to whack the snake in the head with my shoe if he showed up! I finally reached the boat, and I had to get back in the water to climb aboard. As I was getting ready to climb the ladder, that dang snake appeared out of nowhere and slithered right across the top of my ankles. I scurried up the ladder and then had a bit of a meltdown when I knew I was safe. I was done for the day, and I think the rest were too.

When we got back to the marina, we casually asked one of the guys helping to tie up our boat if there were any poisonous snakes in the Lake. "Oh yeah," he says. "But there isn't anything to worry about. Most snakes won't harm you. They swim underwater, and you do not even know that they are around. However, on a rare occasion, if you happen to see a snake that swims with its head out of the water, you would best be getting out of its way because it's the venomous copperhead! But no one hardly ever sees them." Really? Wow! Weren't we the lucky ones?

The Swing's New Home

If any couple who has been married for almost fifty years tells you that they never had an argument, they are lying! No marriage is so perfect that the couple sees eye to eye on everything. If they did, it would be the most boring marriage ever!

There are different ways of showing you're ticked off. Some couples yell and scream, some do the silent treatment, some like a passive-aggressive approach, some just walk away, and some try to sit down and talk things out reasonably, which usually turns into yelling and screaming, passive aggressiveness, or walking away. Ted and I like to spice it up, and we do all three, not at the same time, but we have all three down to a science, and we can pick whichever one suits the situation. I personally like the screaming and yelling approach because it is usually an immediate fix. Get angry, blow up, say things you don't mean, yell about the problem of the day, then rectify it and makeup. The silent treatment can go on for days and days, and the passive-aggressive approach usually does not do any good. And besides, it can be exhausting. Walking away does not solve anything. As we get older, the things that trigger an argument become less and less. As the saying goes, "Don't sweat the small stuff." Don't argue about the small stuff, either. Life is too short. Save it for the really big stuff, like the following story.

As grandparents, you want to give them everything it wasn't possible to give your own children. If you are like us, we were too busy putting food on the table and clothes on the children's backs. By the time the grandkids come along, your billfold has a few more bucks in it, and you've got more time to devote to things the grandkids want.

For instance, when our grandson was about three years old, we bought a swing set kit that we had to put together. It had all the bells and whistles, plus a curly slide and a fort on top. Ted and I decided to put it together ourselves. How hard could it be? Oh, my goodness! What a nightmare! Why couldn't this darn company use all the same size screws and bolts? It took me two hours to separate all the different pieces of hardware and then pray we used the right screw on the correct module. We didn't, of course, so there was a lot of redoing. Ted is not a carpenter. If things need to be put together, I am the one who does it, but this time, I needed a set of muscles to handle all the heavy boards, so he was nominated. It only took us three times as long to put it together as what the box said it should take. We also lost several good tools in the field because, after the yelled obscenities, I would see a nice screwdriver or hammer being flung into the field. I tried to find them all, but there are still a few drill pieces missing.

The look on our grandson's face when he was finally able to try the swing set out was priceless. It was worth every second and every lost tool.

About three years later, we had an adorable granddaughter, and we thought she needed a playhouse. Well, not really "we," as much as "I," but we both agreed we needed to build this playhouse. One night, while sitting in the pool, enjoying an adult beverage, we were discussing how we were going to build this playhouse. In Ted's mind, he was going to build a big box, put a roof on top, and call it done. In my mind, I pictured a replica of the house we live in. It's a great big old two-story farmhouse. Ted, at that point, was still licking his wounds from the swing set, but I caught him in a weak moment, and he agreed. His idea was to get our son-in-law to help, and I told Ted no. Our son-in-law had just started his own construction company, and he was already putting in long, physical hours. And when he got home, I wanted him to enjoy his family. I did not want him to use his spare time doing what he did all day. I had faith in Ted to get it done.

So out came the tools (what was left of them anyway): a tape measure, notepaper to draw the blueprints on, and more paper for a list of supplies. All of this was way above my talents, so I turned Ted loose, and he worked like a house on fire for about a month. Then, he got tired of the project, and I had to prod him along to finish it. When it was finally done, it looked surprisingly good, considering a novice built it. The playhouse did look exactly like our big house, down to the bay windows, white vinyl siding, and green shutters. The inside of the playhouse was two stories, with carpet, overhead lights, a winding staircase, a bed upstairs for sleepovers, and downstairs, it had a TV, a kitchen with a real refrigerator, and a table and chairs. I do believe he must have built it so elaborately, not for the grandkids, but for him if he ever needed to find a new spot to live in case he got in trouble. It sure beat a doghouse! I must say, I was impressed! It had several imperfections, but the grandkids didn't see them, so that is all that mattered.

Oh my, did they have a grand time in it! It was situated right next to the swing set, so their imaginations went crazy! They were pirates one day, outlaws the next, and teachers the day after that. The only trouble was they wanted me to be out there with them all the time, and I had no place to sit. So, when Mother's Day rolled around, Ted gave me a big, old-fashioned porch swing attached to a free-standing frame with a tin roof. We sat it out in the playground, facing the swing set and playhouse. I could sit out there, keep an eye on the kids, read a book, and not get sunburned or rained on because of the roof. It was a perfect setup until, sadly, the grandkids grew up and never played out there again.

The years weren't kind to the swing set. The Indiana weather tortured it with extreme cold and hot temperatures, and the rain and snow started rotting the wood until it was dangerous for any kid to play on. We could fix it back up with new wood, but why? No one was going to play on it, so we decided to drag it over to the big burn pile (almost every farmer has a burn pile somewhere on their property) and set fire to it. I couldn't watch it. It was just too sad. Back at the playground, we still had the playhouse and the old-fashioned swing, just sitting there with its back to the road, staring at the field. It looked weird like that, so I suggested we move it to the other side of the house, in the grass next to our driveway, and we could sit and watch the traffic go past. He begrudgingly agreed.

I love lilacs and always wanted a lilac bush, so when I ran across one, I bought it. I measured where the swing would sit and took into consideration that the lilac bush would grow, so I dug a hole and planted it right in the middle of the yard. It looked rather odd being planted there, but when the swing got moved over there, it would be perfect! I was going to paint the frame of the swing and reinforce a couple of boards that were loose after it got moved.

Out came the tractor with the loading forks attached. All Ted had to do was pick the swing and frame up by sliding the fork prongs under the roof, and he could move it easily to the designated spot. Once he got the swing over there, we realized that the legs were going to sink into the ground. When it was on the playground, it was setting in gravel, so it was fine. Now, the swing would be cockeyed when the legs started sinking into the grass. We needed to sit it on something sturdy. The 16" square stepping stones would be a perfect base! Ted assumed I just wanted four stones, so he jumped in his truck and was off to the building supply store. In reality, I wanted the entire area under the swing covered with stones, which meant he had to buy thirty-something. He was not pleased, but he went along with it.

I could tell he was still miffed when he returned, so I unloaded all the stones myself and started putting them side by side under the swing. For some unknown reason, he decided the swing was in the wrong place, and since I had "planted that stupid bush without using my head," we would not be able to get the mower between the field and the swing. Why did he care? I'm the one who does all the mowing! We said a few more words to each other, and I finally snapped and told him to take the stones back to the store and throw the swing on the burn pile, too!

"No! I'm not going to take them back. Those poor kids that loaded them will hate me if they have to unload them. We're just stuck with a bunch of expensive stones and nowhere to use them!" When he stomped off, muttering under his breath, to the house to get a sandwich, I loaded every one of those stones back onto his truck and told him that those boys get paid to do that, and it was probably their only physical labor they had to do that day.

Our poor son-in-law happened to come over and walk into a bees' nest of Ted and me arguing about the swing. I was yelling to burn the dumb thing, Ted was griping because I did an about-face while our son-in-law was trying to figure out how to make the boards sturdy again without tearing it all apart. This bickering went on for several minutes until Ted asked, "Why did you want to keep the dumb thing in the first place?"

Tears welled up in my eyes as I said, "Because you gave it to me as a Mother's Day gift!" It was now my turn to go stomping into the house. The silent treatment went on for a good four hours until Ted said, rather softly and somewhat apologetically, that he had an idea for what we could do with the swing. "We could take it over to our pond and set it close to the edge of the water so people would have somewhere to sit when they fish!" Hmm… that was actually a brilliant idea!

"I'll help you load it up on the trailer."

"We don't need no stinkin' trailer! I'll just carry it to the pond on the forks of the tractor!"

Our pond is about three miles away, and he was going to drive the tractor with a big old swing hanging in the air in front of him. Really? I guess I wasn't surprised. He's done some whacked-out things, and he usually manages to pull them off, so I just shrugged and said okay.

He had to cross a highway, then turn onto a country road. Country roads around here are not very wide. Two normal vehicles can pass each other, but it usually requires them to slow down so neither one gets off the road and ends up in the ditch. So, he's headed down a county road with a huge swing in the air in front of him. He made it to the first road, but when he tried to turn right, he turned too short and….you guessed it. The swing got dumped in the ditch. He was able to get the swing picked up again and, after a quick inspection, decided it was still in one piece. Off he went again, only to meet a tractor pulling a huge piece of tillage equipment going the opposite way. There was no way that both tractors would be able to pass, so Ted thought he'd better get off the road altogether and sit in the ditch. Once again, the swing went sliding off the forks. He had to wait until the other tractor was completely past and out of the way before he could get the swing picked up again.

Surprisingly, it was still in one piece. The rest of the drive was uneventful, thank goodness. He reached the long drive that went into the woods where our pond was located. He was able to drive about ten feet from the pond, but he hit a tree stump, and the swing slid off the forks again, only this time it landed upside down in the water! Fortunately, the water wasn't very deep, and he was able to pull the swing out and get it set right side up. He says the swing is just fine and in one piece. I'm afraid to go back there and look for fear it's turned into a pile of firewood. I had a question for him, but I didn't dare say it out loud. Why didn't he strap the swing to the forks? Our rule of thumb is "one argument per episode," and we've already spent it earlier that day. Like I said earlier. Save your arguments for the important stuff!

A hobby! Really?

Before you read this story, I just want you to know I am a huge animal lover. All animals! Except maybe spiders and snakes. I have no qualms about throwing a shoe at a spider and praying it lands on it instead of next to it because all that does is make it mad, and then it runs off and hides, just waiting to jump out at you when you have nothing to throw. I wasn't a huge fan of snakes before, but they did not scare me until my lake episode. Now, I am of the opinion that all snakes must die.

Most animals bring me joy. Who can turn their nose up at a six-week-old kitten, all fluffy and cute, playing with its litter mates? I could watch that for hours. My mother used to make up voices for the kittens, and it was hilarious. Puppies are darling, also. Any puppy in the world is cute as a puppy. However, once they grow up, I have seen some mighty ugly dogs, but that does not mean I don't like them. They all have unique personalities. Take our dog, Buckley, for example. He was such a cute little fur ball when we got him, but he already had a distinct personality. He would go flippin' crazy if you touched his neck! Trying to put a collar on him was like catching the Tasmanian Devil with bare hands! He is still that way! I have learned to lay out a long string of lunch meat and attach his collar in midchew. He has many other strange quirks, which means he's psycho, but we love him anyway.

Growing up on a farm, I was not around livestock too much. My dad had cattle for a while when I was really little, but he ended up getting out of the cattle business and just became a grain farmer. I do not think he liked the fact that he had to be home every day to feed the cattle. He enjoyed traveling, and with livestock, that is almost impossible to do.

When I met Ted, he had livestock. Hogs, to be exact. They were not my favorite farm animals, but he liked them, so I tolerated them. After we were married, he continued to raise hogs and sheep for a while, but a job opportunity came along that he could not turn down, so he got rid of the animals.

One day, a few years after he got rid of the hogs and sheep, he came to me and said he really missed taking care of the livestock. He said he would really like to get a couple of cattle. It would give him something to do in the evenings. It would be his hobby. Everybody needs a hobby, right? I thought about it and decided we could do that if he agreed to a couple of stipulations. The first one was that the fences better be strong! I don't want to be chasing any cows down the road or, worse yet, have someone hit a cow with a car. Someone could easily get hurt, not to mention the damage it would do to the vehicle. Good, strong fences were a must! Secondly, this was his hobby, not mine! They were his responsibility! Okay! Now that he agreed to my terms, he suggested, in front of our two children, that we needed to buy four cows instead of two. That way, the kids could each have a cow. They could name it whatever they wanted, and they could go with him in the evenings to take care of them. It was going to be a teachable moment. They were very excited, and off they went to get the cattle. When they returned, the kids told me all about their cows and how they were going to keep them forever.

Once they left the room, I could tell Ted had something to tell me. He skirted around the issue for several minutes, and finally, it came out. "I bought a few more cattle than I had planned. The cattle looked great, and the price was very reasonable. We'll make lots of money on them when I fatten them out and sell them." I sat down and glared at him. "Just how many more cows did you buy?"

"They're purebred Angus, which brings a premium, and I practically stole them!"

"Not what I asked. How many more did you buy?"

"About seventy-six."

Silence. Dead silence. I was speechless! I was also furious, so I guess it was a good thing I was speechless. Pretty soon, though, I found my voice, and I'm sure Ted would have liked for me to go back to being speechless.

After some rather heated words, I realized there was nothing I could do about it. Ted was a spoiled brat who always managed to get his own way, and this time was no exception. After a few days, I cooled down a little bit and reminded him that his agreement still stood. Those fences better hold them, and they are his responsibility, not mine! The kids can help, but I will not! I already had a full-time job and three part-time jobs. Adding cattle to my workload was not happening!

The cattle were content in the big field of alfalfa. There was plenty to go around, so they did not even try to get out. That gave Ted some extra time to double-check the fences.

"So. What are we going to do with them? Just let them eat grass until they die of old age?" Ted looked at me like I had monkeys flying out of my ears.

"Of course not! We are going to breed the cows and sell their calves when they get big enough."

I looked at him closely and asked, "Big enough for what?"

"Big enough for market! We might even send one to the meat packing plant for ourselves. The T-Bones will really be nice and tender!"

"What? No way are you sending any babies of these cows to market! No one is going to eat them!"

"Where do you think the hamburgers, steaks, and roasts in the store come from?"

"Don't be silly. I know the beef is butchered for eating. However, no one is making hamburgers out of our calves!"

"You are getting way ahead of yourself. We will not be dealing with any calves until I find a bull." At this point, I saw major dollar signs. A good bull is expensive.

Ted was bound and determined to drag me into this adventure whether I wanted to be or not. A couple of weeks later, we visited a farm that raised and sold Angus bulls. There were about thirty-five to forty huge bulls in this pasture, and the gentleman invited us to walk around in the pasture and check them out closely. Really? Won't we get trampled? He assured us they were all used to people and were docile. We climbed the fence and started strolling through the herd. Ted was looking for certain characteristics. I was trying to figure out a good name for them. I noticed one particular bull that kept staring at me. He inched closer, and as I stepped back. The more I went backwards, the closer he got. I was beginning to become very wary of this bull.

He either loved me or hated me, but I wasn't going to hang around in an open field to find out. I walked very quickly to their barn and stood with my back against the wall, away from the bull. I stayed there for about fifteen minutes and decided it must have been my imagination. I stepped away from the barn and peeked around the corner. Yikes! Peeking around the opposite corner was the bull staring me right in the eye! This guy was giving me the heebie-jeebies, so I climbed back over the fence and stood next to the truck. The next thing I knew, Mr. Bull was standing next to the fence, still staring at me! I got in the truck just in case the fence was not strong enough to hold him. All this was going on while Ted was roaming around the field, inspecting all the other bulls. When he came back towards the truck, he saw Mr. Bull and looked him over once, then twice, then three times.

Of all the stinkin' bulls in the whole lot, he decided on Mr. Bull! "Didn't you see the way he was looking at me?"

"No. Why?" I explained that I was being pursued, or courted, by this big guy, and I was not going to be around to find out which it was!

"It's all your imagination. Maybe he likes your perfume or something." It was the "Something" I was worried about. Ted assured me that I wouldn't be around this four-legged Casanova anyway since I made it perfectly clear I wasn't going to be involved.

So, Mr. Bull came to our farm, and we introduced him to his new harem. It took a while before the lady cows warmed up to him, but little by little, there was a lot of romance going on. I think I actually saw a smile on his face! He was happy with his ladies, but whenever I happened to walk through the field, he came running.

All was going well until late fall when the alfalfa was gone. The cows needed to be moved across the road into the barn lot, where we would feed and water them until spring and where they had plenty of warm shelter inside the barn.

Ted went down every evening and put feed and corn in their feeders. It got so that the cows knew the sound the buckets made and came running to the feeder. "They are so smart," I said. "How cute!" Ted would rub them on their heads as they ate, and they all began acting like big pets.

Ted's job involved attending farm shows during the winter, where he staffed a booth, along with several other men, promoting the grain-handling products they sold. He had done this for several years and became good friends with all the other men. It was a four-day event, so he had to stay in a hotel. After the show was closed for the day, all the guys would grab some supper together, then end up in one of the hotel rooms, where they played cards, drank a few adult beverages, and basically told huge lies to each other.

When show season rolled around and knowing that Ted was going to be gone for several nights, I became curious about the cows. Was he going to put out enough food that would last them until he got back? Not hardly! They would eat it all the first night, get sick, then starve the rest of the week. These girls did not know how to pace themselves. So, guess who was elected to take care of them while he was gone? Yep! The person who said she would have nothing to do with them. Dang it, anyway! Ted had me between a rock and a hard place, and he knew it.

The night before he left, I went down to the cattle lot with him so he could show me what I needed to do. It was a cold night, and you could see the breath of each cow. It was a bit tricky walking over the frozen footprints the cows had made earlier. Ted started across the feedlot with two big buckets of corn. The cows ran to the feeder, just waiting for him to pour it in. After a few pats on their heads, off Ted went to check the water and make sure it wasn't frozen. I was busy writing all these steps down. No cow was going to die on my watch!

The next morning, Ted was headed off to the show for four glorious days! Don't get me wrong. I did miss him when he was gone, but those four days gave me the opportunity to do some deep cleaning. There was nothing sacred. Closets, drawers, and anything that did not move got a good going-over. The time also afforded me the chance to pitch lots and lots of stuff without Ted being there to say, "You're not going to throw that away, are you?" I filled up our dumpsters, and it was hauled away before Ted got home. The funny thing was that he didn't miss anything I pitched, so it was a win/win for me. It was late afternoon, so I thought I had better get the cattle taken care of before it got dark. Everything went fairly uneventfully. I patted myself on the back and went back home. I walked in just in time to hear the weather forecast. It was going to warm up above freezing and rain. Oh lovely.

The next morning, it was raining, and the temperature was thirty-eight degrees. It was a good day to stay in the house and attack a couple of closets. Once again, it was getting close to evening, and it was time for me to get the cattle fed and watered. It had stopped raining, thank goodness. When I got to the cattle lot, I saw a sea of mud between me and the feeder. I was grateful I had slipped on my tall rubber boots. The water tank was overflowing thanks to the rain. Check that task off the list. Next came the food. I filled both buckets with corn and carried them inside the gate of the feedlot. Oh my! Not only was it mud, it was deep mud! I made my way very slowly, picking the high spots to step on that were peeking out of the mud. Unfortunately, the farther I got, the worse it got.

I stepped forward, only to have my boot stuck in the mud. Drat! I managed to pull my boot out of that murky mess and get my foot back in it. I took a step with my other foot, and that boot also got sucked off my foot! Now I'm really in a predicament because the cows heard the bucket and took off for the feeder. I stepped again; the boot stayed behind. I get the bright idea to sit the bucket down in front of me and stand in the bucket. Then I put the other bucket in front of the first one, and I stood in that one. I am a genius!

I'm walking across the shin-deep mud lot, using the buckets of corn! It was working great until the cows grew impatient, waiting for their supper. They decided to come to me! Cows were surrounding me from all sides, trying to get the corn underneath my socked feet. Cows were pushing other cows out of the way, each trying to get their share. Suddenly, I felt a tug on my sock. One of the cows was eating my sock! My toes were in that sock, and I was scared to death they were going to be eaten, too! This is when I started screaming! Screaming at the top of my lungs! Sadly, no one was around to hear. The corn was getting lower in the buckets. That meant I was getting lower also. Now, I was fearful that they would push against me and snap my legs right off. There was only one thing to do. I stepped out of the buckets of corn and into shin-high cold mud.

I managed to wiggle my way through the mess of cows, only getting my foot stepped on once, and made it to the safety of the gate. I turned around to take inventory. The buckets had been emptied, and now they were rolling them around in the mud. At that point, I didn't care. I managed to grab my boots as I slowly slopped past. My feet were ten times bigger than normal due to the mud caked on them. I was not going to put those feet in the boots, so I walked over to a grassy area, took off my socks, tried to scrape some of the mud off my legs with my hands, and stood there looking like a mud monster. My feet were numb at this point, but I knew I had better get some warm water on them soon. I sure didn't want to climb in my van, still covered in mud, so I took my pants and my heavy coat off, turned them right side out, and threw them in the back of the van. I climbed into the driver's seat with just a T-shirt and no pants. I wasn't sure if

I could drive or not since my feet were still numb, but I headed home, praying I wouldn't have a flat tire.

Once I got home, I stood in the warm shower for what seemed like an hour with chunks of mud going down the drain. Finally, the mud was all gone, and I was warm again. My feet were a nice bright pink, and now I had the sensation of needles pricking my feet. Thousands of needles.

Ted always calls me every morning and evening when he's away. When the phone rang, I hobbled to answer it. "Hey beautiful! How's it going?" (He always calls me beautiful. The poor man either has bad eyes or somehow, he had heard me screaming at the cows an hour earlier) If he had known just what I went through, I doubt that he would have called, but he did, and I answered his question very loudly! In fact, I was yelling so loud that the rest of the guys in the room heard me. They were laughing out loud at how much trouble Ted was in. I unloaded on him as I recounted every horrible moment. I have a feeling he was laughing too. Now, every time I see one of those guys, they are all too eager to remind me of that night.

The cows stuck around a while longer, and they all started having calves. One particular calf was so large it actually paralyzed the momma. She couldn't stand up. The vet said it was probably a temporary thing, and she should come out of it in a month or so. However, that was not getting her little baby to nurse. Ted, being the problem-solver that he is, came up with an outstanding idea. He rigged a harness up that went around the momma, and then he jacked her up until she was standing. That gave the calf the ability to nurse until he was full, and then Ted would lower her back down. One day, he and his buddy were on their way to a service call, and they stopped to raise the cow so the calve could drink. The cow got off center somehow, and she toppled over, right on top of Ted. Thank goodness his friend was there to help.

If he hadn't been, it was hard telling how long Ted would have laid under that cow. I would like to say that he was unharmed, but unfortunately, the cow broke his back. Well, not his entire back. She broke a couple of his vertebra, which ended up needing surgery. He healed fairly quickly, and I think he was surprised that the cattle were still there. I should have sold them while he was in the hospital, but I did not. Ted hung on to the cows for quite a while longer, but I could tell they were beginning to become a chore, not a hobby. One day, he decided to sell them. That was one of the best decisions he made. I think he was sad, and I tried to sympathize with him, but inside, I was secretly doing cartwheels!

Firebugs

Since the beginning of time, Man has had a fascination with fire. After, of course, they figured out what fire was and how to achieve it. I think it must have been a lightning strike that started fire. Who, in their right mind, would sit all day, rubbing two sticks together or smacking two rocks against each other just for the fun of it? I am sure they were bored—no TV, internet, books to read, no phones, or Facebook. I'm surprised they didn't just die of boredom. Except for drawing stick figures on a cave wall or chasing a random dinosaur now and then, what else could they do? I bet they were grouchy and hungry, too. I have never seen a nice caveman, except for Fred Flintstone and Barney Ruble. Thank goodness fire came along when it did, or we wouldn't be here! Fire gave them something to do. The biggest being cooking that dinosaur that they chased earlier. I bet that helped with the grouchiness, also.

"What's for supper, dear? I'm starving. We've invented a Fire Department, just in case one of our fires gets out of hand. I helped stomp out three fires today!"

"We're having a T-Rex rump roast and a bucket of berries."

"Again? We have that all the time."

I wonder if they had Dinosaur Helper?

When my son was three, he was fascinated with fire. So much so that he lit some papers on fire in his wastepaper basket in his room; he came running out of his room, screaming "HELP!" and throwing three-ounce Dixie Cups full of water on the fire. Fortunately, he got it put out, but I never figured out how he got the lighter and how strong his fingers were to use it. I struggle with lighters myself. I had the lighter put way up high in a cabinet out of his reach. Well, apparently, it wasn't out of his reach. He climbed like a billy goat and was fast as lightning. Oh, the stories I could tell about him! But that's for another day.

Realizing his fascination almost burned down our house. I decided, with my supervision, of course, he was now the guy in charge of burning the trash. He could light as many papers on fire as he wanted, as long as he kept it in our trash barrel. Man, did he have a blast! He thought he was the big man on campus until I told him that part of the job was to take the trash to the trash barrel. Suddenly, his joy of burning stuff stopped. But my little plan worked, and he quit messing around with the lighter.

My son got his fire addiction from his dad. Ted loves to set fires. He will offer to take out the burnable trash just so he can set it on fire. Then he stands and watches it burn until everything is gone. He's very eager to burn boxes I have saved all year for Christmas presents. I came home one day, and he had burned every box and was proud of himself for doing so! So now I must supervise him too, just so he doesn't burn something I want to keep.

Many years ago, one of our farms had about 150 old tires piled up in the back of the field down in a ravine. Obviously, the farm's previous owner was a bit eccentric while he was alive. We then acquired the property. It was only about two miles from our house, and it had lots of tillable acreage and lots of pasture. Perfect for the stupid cows I wrote about in the last story. Everything was peachy except for those ugly tires and a dilapidated barn.

One night, and I stress it was many, many years ago, just in case the statute of limitations is questioned, he decided to burn said tires. No one would see the fire because they were located over a hill and in a ravine. He chose nighttime because there wouldn't be any traffic going past, which would mean fewer curious people wondering where the horrendous odor was coming from. Have you ever smelled a burning tire? If you haven't, consider yourself incredibly lucky. One tire will tear your eyes up, and your nose will jump right off your face and run away.

In case you are wondering, burning tires is a big no-no, but Ted, being the frugal man that he is, just took it as a suggestion. He said he figured that it was for people in towns and cities, not us rural folk. If we were to take them to Waste Management, it would cost a fortune because they charge for every tire. He certainly wasn't going to spend that kind of money getting rid of an eyesore. He could take care of it himself. He could hardly contain himself all day, anticipating what he had planned for that night. When darkness finally came, there was not a star in the sky, and the moon wasn't visible.

"Great! This will be perfect! No one will be able to see anything as dark as it is." I rubbed my forehead because I could feel yet another major headache coming on. I get a lot of headaches, but the really bad ones are usually Ted-induced. I was not going with him because I didn't want to be an accessory to the crime. This baby was all on him. He could take 100 percent of the credit and praise for cleaning up such a mess, or he could also go to jail.

I waited four hours for him to come home. Four hours, and he still had not shown up. I wanted to know what was going on, and I didn't want to know. It was 1:00 in the morning, and he finally called. He said he was going to be a while because he was on his way to town, which is seven miles away. "What on earth are you going to town for at this hour?"

"You haven't been outside, have you?"

"No, I haven't."

"Go look out the window. There is the most beautiful full moon tonight, and there must be a gazillion stars shining brighter than ever! The clouds went away, and it's as bright as daylight out here! The tires are putting out a lot of black smoke, and it's going high in the sky and headed for town. I'm going to see how far away I can see the smoke."

"Really? You're kidding me, right?"

I was getting drowsy before he called, but I was wide awake now! After about forty-five minutes, he called me again. "You are not going to believe this. (A phrase that he uses often). The smoke has wrapped itself around the courthouse tower and is headed to the interstate!" We had people tell us later that they saw it twenty miles away!

You cannot put it out when a pile of rubber tires is burning. It just must burn itself out. They also put out the blackest, most pungent smoke you will ever see or smell. Ted headed back to the crime scene, hoping the clouds would come back and, if he got lucky enough, they would drop two inches of rain. Even if the tires continued to burn, at least the rain would stop the smoke. No such luck. He sat in his truck, watching the debacle, when he started noticing all these cars and trucks coming into the driveway. They must have been following the smoke! It was like following a rainbow to where it starts and finding a pot of gold! Only this was not a pot of gold! They would turn around and leave once they saw that it wasn't a building burning down. Their curiosity was satisfied. But the stream of vehicles coming and going went on way past dawn.

Ted had fallen asleep in his truck, and when he woke up, he was hoping the tires were gone, which meant the evidence was also gone. Ha! Did you know that rubber tires burn forever? The entire end of the county stunk! We were absolutely shocked when the sheriff didn't show up. I'm sure people reported it, but I'm also sure the sheriff just shook his head. He more than likely said, "That's probably Ted. He's a really nice guy, but he tends to do unorthodox things. We'll take care of it." They never did talk to him, knowing it was probably a waste of their time anyway. The sheriff probably told his deputy, "He'll more than likely do something again soon, and we'll talk to him then."

The tires smoldered for days into the following week! Finally, they were gone. I prayed Ted learned his lesson, but my prayer went unanswered. It wasn't too much later that he decided to burn down the barn. It was an eyesore, too. After all, the cattle were gone, and it was not being used for anything anymore. It was in sad shape. It needed several coats of paint, a new roof, and new doors. That would cost a fortune, and then it would still be unused. So why bother?

"Let's just burn it down!" Thinking he got away with the tires, he picked a bright Saturday morning when the sun was shining and set it on fire. Whoosh! It was ablaze and gone before you could blink twice! All that dried-out old timber burned quickly. Since it was much closer to the road, everyone could see the flames shooting high into the air. A volunteer fireman showed up and wanted to see Ted's permit. Ted did not know he needed a permit to burn his barn on his property. The fireman warned him and told him the next time he had a building to burn, he was to call them, and they would schedule a controlled burn that they did themselves. Apparently, they like playing with matches also!

Little did we know that as Ted was trying to give up his pyromania addiction, our daughter had picked up the torch! (See what I did there?)

Our daughter was a sophomore in high school, and it was fall break. I think everyone has heard of toilet papering, where kids sneak up to your house at night and cover your trees and bushes with toilet paper. A roll of toilet paper gets thrown over the top of the tree or branch; it unwinds itself from the roll, and then you tear it off and start another tree. Can you imagine the look on the checkout girl's face when the kids walk in and buy a case of cheap toilet paper? No one has ever thrown Charmin or Cottonelle in a tree. Save yourself some money and use the scratchy one-ply stuff. Another unspoken rule is the more popular you are, the more toilet paper gets applied to your yard. My rule, as I told my daughter, is if we get toilet papered, you are the one that will clean it up.

Some brainchild came up with an idea to shred the rolls of toilet paper into tiny pieces and scatter them over the yard. Once the dew came down and made it wet, you instantly had paper mache all over your grass. That was a pain to clean up.

My daughter and a group of her friends paid a visit to several people over the fall break week. When I woke up that Friday morning and looked out our window, I was met with a scene from a Christmas movie. Not only did all our trees hang full of toilet paper, but our grass was covered, too. It looked like a winter wonderland, only it was sixty degrees. When the daughter woke up on her last day of fall break, I told her she needed to eat breakfast, and then she had a job to do outside. She took one look out the window, and I thought she was going to pass out. I heard her mutter something under her breath, but it was best that I didn't ask her to repeat it. She dilly-dallied around in the house for a while, then found the lighter and went to work. She would walk up to a toilet paper end and flick the lighter. The paper ignited and burned all the way to the other end! I thought it was pure genius!

She got rid of all the toilet paper in the trees in record time. But there was a mess on the grass to clean up as well. I figured she would have to use a rake, and it was going to take her a while because we have a two-acre yard. She disappeared, and then out of the garage, she came with our lawn tractor and the grass sweeper hooked behind. She would make a lap, and the sweeper picked up every bit of that paper. Pure genius again! When she got done, there was not one sign of the mischief that happened the night before.

Finally, Monday rolled around, and it was time to get back to school. I opened the front door so she could see the school bus coming down the road. When I opened the door, I was met with the lovely smell of someone starting up their wood stove. It was a chilly morning, so I didn't blame them. I was secretly wishing I had a fireplace to cozy up to. Unfortunately, I had no time for wishful thinking, I had to get to work. Ted and I both worked right across from where we lived in my father's grain-handling business. I sat in the front office with a big picture window facing our house. I happened to glance out after dinner, and there were flames shooting out of the top of the tree! I called 9-1-1, and they sent the local Volunteer Fire Department.

They got there quickly enough, but when they climbed out of their trucks, that's when the bedlam started. I kid you not…two guys actually got into an argument about who was climbing the ladder and who got to hold the hose! As they were bickering, another guy grabbed the hose and walked around the tree. As he walked, he somehow got the hose wrapped around the ladder, and the guy on the ladder was doing circus tricks to keep from falling off. I secretly named these guys Larry, Curly, and Moe. Finally, after the fire was extinguished, they began looking at the tree. The fire had literally gutted the trunk! But what caused the fire? All three guys were playing detective, looking for the starting point. They all agreed that the fire started when three branches came together above the main trunk. However, they could not figure out what started it. But I knew.

The scenario we came up with is this. Whoever did their decorating job on us Thursday night must have pitched a roll of toilet paper up, and it landed right in the valley where all three branches met. When our daughter lit the end of the paper, it burned up into that valley and burned and burned, then probably smoldered for a while. The roll was on fire for so long, though, that it caught the tree on fire and continued to burn its way down inside the trunk. It took three full days for the fire to incinerate the inside. Monday morning, when I opened the door and told Ted that someone started their woodstove and it smelled like a campfire, it was us, not knowing there was a small blaze happening inside the tree.

I loved that tree. It was an incredibly old tree. If that tree could talk, it would certainly have some marvelous stories to tell! It stood in front of our house and provided shade for the porch. I loved to open the window and listen to the breeze blowing through the leaves. That tree was there long before our house was built in 1885. In fact, I bet the Indians took naps under that tree because it was so inviting. Indians? Yes, there was a tribe of Indians that lived on the property I grew up on. We would find arrowheads, wooden mallets, broken clay dishes, and more. I told my daughter that the poor tree withstood tornadoes, blizzards, drought, floods, and the

Civil War. But it was no match for her! (See what I did there? Match?)

The next thing we needed to do was cut the tree down before it fell on the house. I wanted to hire a qualified logger, but Ted decided we did not need to cut it down immediately. "It seems to be still living, so let's just leave it alone." The real reason was that he didn't want to pay someone for something he thought he could do.

Amazingly, it stood for a couple of years! Then, one day, a storm brewed up with gale-force winds. It was more than the tree could take, and down it came on the corner of our house. It wasn't nearly as bad as it could have been, but the house still needed repair work.

A friend and his sons happened to drive past and saw the mess. They kept right on going but soon returned, armed with chainsaws and handsaws. With their help, we got the tree cut up and hauled away. Although, we were left with a huge, splintered stump in front of the house. I said we needed to find someone with a stump grinder and get rid of it. Ted had a better idea, of course. He poured kerosene all over the top of the stump, let it soak in, and then poured more. He did that several times until it was time to light the match! He acted sad over the loss of our tree, but I think he was doing cartwheels in his head because he got to burn the stump. And burn, it did!

It burned and burned and smoldered. More kerosene then burned some more. This wasn't a one-day job. This stump was huge, so it took many days until it finally burned in half, leaving each side of the stump still standing. I asked him if we could please get a stump grinder and finish it off. "No way! This is a quest!" It went from a simple job to a huge challenge!

One Sunday morning, he decided he was going to finish off the stumps since there were now two big sides still standing. He doused the wood with kerosene again, then he left for a while, and when he came back, he had a big tire still on the rim. He tossed it in the middle of the stumps and poured kerosene on it. I asked him to not do it, but he said it was the perfect time because the wind was blowing away from the road. Besides, on Sunday morning, how much traffic can there be? I guess he hadn't read the paper or listened to the radio because a huge festival was happening in a small town south of us. The best way to get there was the highway that passed our house. He didn't see the traffic going south on Saturday. It was RVs and campers galore, one after another.

He clicked the lighter, and BOOM, the tire, and the stumps burst into flames. He was quite proud of himself as they burned, the heavy, smelly smoke blowing away from the road. The fire kept going for four to five hours, and it was doing the job. The flames went down, and it was just smoldering, so we went back inside the house. As we were sitting in the living room, enjoying a peaceful Sunday afternoon, we heard a car honk. Shortly after that, another car honked. We peered out the window to see what the ruckus was about. The wind had shifted. Actually, it had done a complete about-face, and the black smoke was blowing across the highway, not up in the air but hanging low to the ground, about car height.

I said, "Well, that can't be good! Someone is going to have an awful wreck because they can't see, and it will be our fault!" Ted rushed out, grabbed the hose, and doused the fire. He drenched it well so it would not smolder and pop up a few days later. At least he was paying attention, considering the tree fiasco. After everything settled down, all we were left with was two stumps and a half-burned tire with a charred rim. He went into the house to plan his next attack.

I finally had to tell him there would be no more fires, no more tires. I was hiding the matches and lighters, and I would take care of the stumps. We now have a lovely three-tiered flower garden in our front yard. We built it big enough to circle the stumps, stuck a tall American flag in the top tier, and encased all the tiers in landscaping bricks. It looks nice, and one could ever tell that two stumps are still buried underneath. I wanted to tell Ted that hiring a guy to get rid of the stump would have been a lot cheaper than what we ended up doing, but I did not think I should rub salt in the wound.

I did have one episode where I became the perpetrator and the victim! It was springtime, and the tractors, tillage equipment, and planters were kicking up dust everywhere you looked. Everyone in the family was helping get the crops planted, including my son-in-law and daughter. Everyone except me. I was all by myself, and I planned on getting a lot of yard work accomplished. We have three big ornamental grass plants next to the side of the pool. They are pretty in the summer because they get tall and hide the wall of the pool and give it some character. However, the tall grass dies when late fall comes, and it just stands there, looking ugly. Every fall, I told myself I was going to get rid of that grass so it wouldn't look so ugly during the winter, but I never seemed to get around to it. So, I usually just do it in the springtime.

A few years before this, I cut it level with the ground, but the grass blew all over my yard and landscaping rocks. I never was able to get it all picked up. The next year, I put a big garbage bag over the top of the grass before I cut it off, and it did capture some of it, but a lot still escaped and blew all over the yard again. The following year, I got the bright idea to burn it. The first grass plant burned completely to the ground with nothing blowing in my yard. Kudos to me! I stepped to the next grass plant, did the same thing, and then proceeded to the third plant. They all burned to the ground, and it always worked perfectly. Sometimes, I surprise myself with how clever I am!

This year, I armed myself with the lighter, ready to get rid of the ugly, brown grass and then get on with the rest of the yard work. I lit the first plant, and it burned quickly to the ground. I set the second plant on fire, and instead of waiting for it to burn out, I went ahead and lit the third plant. About that time, I noticed a breeze starting to blow. I glanced at the second burning plant; the breeze had blown the grass right next to the pool wall, and the outside part of our pool liner was melting! I jumped into action and was able to pull the grass away from the pool, but somehow, I managed to set my clothes on fire!

I was wearing some lightweight shorts and a top that started melting into my skin as soon as the heat got close. I jumped back and started stripping right there in the yard, next to the highway, where every Tom, Dick, and Harry driving past could see me! At the time, I was not so much worried about the people seeing me as much as I was worried about the clothes that were melting my skin! There I am, shorts and shirt smoldering on the ground, with me standing in my underwear, trying to pick melted cloth off my legs! I finally came to my senses, ran into the house, and doctored my burns with ointment.

I went back outside, after putting different clothes on, of course, to inspect the damage done to the pool liner. The grass was all gone, and there was a huge, charred spot on the wall of the pool and blue, melted vinyl dripping down the side wall. Man, Ted is not going to be a happy camper about this! I had to fess up and tell him what I did when he got home that night. It was the right thing to do, especially since I couldn't disguise his melted mess. Besides, he would wonder why I smelled like burning rubber.

The next day, I called our local pool supply store and had them come out and look at the liner and sidewall. I was afraid we would have to replace the entire liner. Fortunately, he said he thought the liner would hold up since all the damage was to the outside. Boy, was I relieved! Pool liners are not that cheap, and it's a major headache to replace them. But I was stuck with that ugly, charred place on the side of the pool, and everyone driving past would be able to see it. So, I did what needed to be done. I found a can of white spray paint and painted over the black spot and the melted drips of vinyl that I could not get off. No one will ever know what happened that day, but I learned my lesson. From now on, I will cut the grass off, even if it makes a mess in my yard.

Banking is Not For The Weak

When our daughter was in high school, she was on the varsity softball team. She had played softball since she could swing a bat. She loved the sport, and she was good at it. In fact, she still plays in a co-ed league just for fun. The first year she started playing, I took her to practice, and one of the mothers informed the rest of us that the person who was going to be the coach backed out, and she was hoping one of us would step up and take their place. She pleaded with us to do it so we wouldn't let the girls down. Knowing how talented Ted is in softball and what a great temperament he has, I knew he'd make an excellent coach for these girls. So, I raised my hand and said, "I bet Ted would do it!" All the rest of the mothers clapped and said how happy they were that Ted was going to coach. Now, I just needed to tell Ted that he was their new coach.

"You're kidding me, right?" I shook my head no, and to help me win him over, our daughter sat on his lap, looked at him with puppy-dog eyes, and said, "Please, Daddy?" That's my girl! He was on board from that day on! Ted coached those girls every year and loved it more with each passing season. He taught them a lot, but our daughter really benefited from it because she was a force to be reckoned with on the pitcher's mound. Her batting was amazing, too. When she was sixteen, her days of playing in the county league were over, which meant that Ted's days of coaching were over. She was so good when she got into high school that she made the varsity team as a freshman.

In her sophomore year, a "nationally known photography company" came to the school to take pictures for the yearbook of all the sporting teams. She had brought home a form to fill out if we wanted any pictures, and if we did, we were to enclose the check and form in the envelope. I got the "A" package, which came with one 8x10 for us, two 5x7s for both sets of grandparents, and a bunch of wallets for all her friends. The whole package only cost $12.00, which I thought was very reasonable, even back then. I sent the $12.00 check to her the next day. Little did I know how much that was going to cost me!

A few days later, Ted had to go to a funeral for one of his relatives. I had something I had to do, so I didn't go with him, and as it turned out, it was a good thing I didn't. While in the line at the visitation, he saw a few cousins he had not seen in ages, and as they talked, they all decided to go to a local restaurant and grab some supper and talk some more. He needed cash because back then, credit cards had not hit their popularity as they have now. He drove up to the ATM machine at our bank and punched in $50.00. Out spit a pink paper (pink is not a good color if you're doing a bank transaction). It said he could not have any money because we were overdrawn. Really? That can't be! He punched in a different button again, and out popped another pink slip that gave him the balance in our checking account. It read that we had a negative balance of $118,433,70! He nearly passed out behind the wheel! He wondered what the heck I had done to put us this far in the red. He went ahead and met his cousins at the restaurant, but all he ordered was a Coke because that was all the cash he had. He made up some lame excuse that he had already eaten a big supper. Needless to say, he did not stay awfully long.

When he got home, he showed me the pink slips. I was flabbergasted! I am the one who takes care of paying the bills and making the deposits, and I knew, to the penny, how much we had in our checking account. We had $1,578.30 left after I paid all our bills. I swore to him that I didn't know what happened. I convinced Ted that those pink slips could not possibly be correct, and he believed me, thank goodness. We both figured the ATM machine was messed up and was spitting out errors to everybody. I remember both of us even laughing about it, wondering what I could have bought for all the money! I told him I would call the bank in the morning and get it straightened out.

When morning came, I did not have to call the bank. The bank called me! The person on the other end of the line said, "Is this Mrs. Hahn?"

"Yes."

"I'm so-and-so from so-and-so bank, and I need to talk to you about your account. It seems to be overdrawn by quite a hefty sum. Until you make a deposit that will get you out of the negative, we will not honor any more checks, and the ATM will not be accessible to you either."

I told her, "Funny! I was just going to call you. Ted tried to take some cash out of the ATM, and all he got were these little pink papers that told us some nonsense about being overdrawn. Your ATM must have a glitch in it."

I was met with a small bit of silence, then a very curt, "No. Our ATM is working just fine. When I pull up your account, it clearly shows that a check for $120,012.00 was just processed, and it was taken out of your account."

"I did no such thing! I know exactly how much we have in the account because I have a slight case of OCD, and I always balance the account To! The! Penny!"

Now, remember, this was many years ago, long before banking online, depositing checks with your phone, and having instant access to your account on your mobile device. This was when some of the tellers were still using calculators or extremely basic computers that they could play Pong on in their slow time.

She ended the conversation with, "I trust you will be in to rectify this matter?" I told her I'd be in shortly, and she just hung up on me. No goodbye, have a lovely day. We value your business, not anything. I guess she did not value my business since our names were flashing red everywhere.

As I walked through the bank doors, I was a walking mess. I was furious, scared, puzzled, and then furious again. Fortunately, the bank manager, whom I knew fairly well, asked me if she could help me. I told her Yes, and she said to step into her office.

"What can I help you with?"

"I just got a call from someone here who said we were overdrawn by quite a bit, and I need to know what's going on." As I was saying that, the lady I talked to on the phone earlier walked past the office door, overheard what I said, turned around, and came back.

"Oh. I'm so glad you brought in a deposit. The bank really frowns on accounts that overdraw."

Well, duh! (I thought it but didn't say it.)

The lady behind the desk told her she would handle it, and the condescending one did an about-face and walked away. I glanced at the manager, and she just rolled her eyes as she walked away. She's my kind of person! Now, we'll get it figured out.

"Humm… let's see here." She looked up my account, and because she was the bank manager, she had access to whom the checks were written. "It looks to me like all the checks are fairly small except for this one for $120,012.00."

"I've never written a check that huge!" By now, I have tears in my eyes. "Can you tell me who the check was written to?"

"Yes. It says you wrote it to 'nationally known photography studio!'"

"I did not! I wrote them a check for $12.00!"

As she studied the screen, she got a big smile on her face. "Do you know what happened? This photography studio is such a large company they key in their own checks because there are so many. This means they take the bank tellers out of the equation and do the depositing themselves. I bet whoever was keying in your $12.00 check got interrupted, and she keyed in $12.00 twice, which would make it $120,012.00! I will get it straightened out for you. It may take a couple of days."

I was so relieved; I couldn't wait to tell Ted! He was relieved also but a little more pensive than me. He was worried about how long it would take to correct the mess-up because this could really ruin our credit!

We waited for the phone call that would release us from debt prison for the rest of the week. We had about $5.49 cash between the two of us, and I needed $2.50 of that for our daughter's school lunch. Fortunately, I had a package of bologna and some bread in the freezer that Ted could eat for lunch, and we were fortunate enough to have plenty of meat in the freezer and vegetables from the garden. The trouble was that we couldn't get cash out of the ATM, and we did not dare write a check because it would bounce from here to the ocean. If only they had bounced that $120,012.00 check instead of overdrawing us!

Adding insult to injury, an official letter came in the mail from the bank. It was informing us of the overdraft, and they would be charging us $25.00 and then interest per day until we rectified it! I called my friend at the bank, and she chuckled and then assured me she would get it taken care of.

We waited for a few more days. Ted needed money to buy gas. We searched the couch cushions and tore the car apart, looking for any spare change we could find. We produced about $3.00 in change, a comb, a mini can of hairspray, a fuzz-covered Lifesaver, and a Barbie shoe. Then I remembered the penny jar. We had enough pennies that Ted could at least get gas for the week.

I was beginning to get worried that it would not be straightened out. It had been ten days. A couple of days later, I got a call from the bank manager. She apologized for taking such a long time. She said the red tape to wade through was a nightmare, but there wasn't any way around it. "However," she said. "I'm going to put the money back into your account from the bank. We have a slush fund available for things of this nature." Two things came to my mind instantly. Number one… why in the heck didn't they use this slush fund immediately after they saw what happened? And number two… who keeps that sum of money in a slush fund? But okay. I will take it.

I'm the type of person that doesn't let sleeping dogs lie. I must know details, and I want answers, and I want people to take responsibility for their mess-ups. I called the "nationally known photography studio," located in Tennessee, and told them what they did. I got passed around like yesterday's meatloaf. No one wanted to talk to me. Finally, one poor guy took the call. I suspected it was the janitor. He passed me on to another department. I got to talk to the receptionist and explained that I wanted to talk to the person who did this to us and explain the hardship she put us through. She might have even ruined our credit, and I just wanted an "I'm sorry" out of them. I was met with dead silence. I would bet you $100.00 that the receptionist put me on hold, told everybody who I was and what I wanted, and they burst into hysterical laughter. When she came back on the phone, she said it was impossible to say who did it and hung up.

All I wanted was some sort of an apology, but it was clear that I was not going to get it. I grumbled and griped until finally, Ted said to just let it go.

Karma is a funny thing. Sometimes it happens quickly, and sometimes it takes a long time. With today's technology, the world has changed drastically, sometimes for the good and sometimes not. The phones of today take amazing pictures, so no one needs a professional photographer unless it's a wedding or something else huge. Today, I would have been able to see what happened the day it happened. It would have been straightened out immediately, and Ted could have eaten dinner with his cousins. One good thing came out of the whole ordeal. We did find the lost Barbie shoe!

May I See Your Driver's License, Please?

When you're a kid growing up on a farm, you know how to drive before you take a driver's training course in order for you to get your license. I remember driving the pickup truck around on the farm helping Dad with many projects. Actually, I was a rather good driver! I didn't drive the big grain trucks at the time for two reasons. One…my feet could not reach the pedals, and two…it was a manual transmission, and I wasn't comfortable shifting the gears. But I sure could drive an automatic!

At the same time, I drove the pickup truck (only on the farm, I reiterate!) Dad had me drive the tractors, especially in the spring. I usually was the one that they stuck doing the discing (tilling the ground before it could be planted) since Dad could put it in the right gear, and I could control the speed with the throttle. He would open the field up, which means he made a path around the edge and then started me at one end of the field. He would ride a couple of rounds with me, then turn me loose! I was so proud that I was doing something that was helpful.

When I was in the fifth grade, he rode a couple of rounds with me, and when I got to the end, I slowed the throttle way down. I remember Dad saying, "You don't need to slow it down that much when you come to the end. Just slow it a little, make the turn, drop the disc, and then speed up. Okey-dokey! I can do that! I have always liked to go fast!

We got to the end of the field; I stopped, he climbed off so he could return to his planter, and off I went. Everything went great for about three hours. Then it happened. I was feeling rather overconfident, so I thought I didn't have to slow the tractor down at all. I started the turn, and the tractor slid sideways. That was bad enough, but I slid right into a wire fence and kept going, getting the disc blades all tangled up with the fence. When I finally got the tractor stopped, I climbed down to inspect what I had done, hoping that no one saw it. I thought I could get the fencing undone from the disc, but I still had to explain why there was a big hole in the fence. Dad was always patient with me and very forgiving, so I knew I would get a lecture at the worst. As I was walking to the shop to get the tools that I needed to cut the fence, I glanced back at what I had done. I stopped dead in my tracks! There was a fence post sticking straight out in the front of the tractor. It looked like someone had thrown a spear and stabbed it! Ohhhh…that is not good!

I walked back to the tractor to look closer at the damage. What the heck is all that water doing on the ground? I thought to myself. Man, I hope it's not what I think it is, but it was. The fence post had impaled the radiator. Needless to say, when Dad saw it from the next field over, he came running. The very first thing he did was ask me if I was all right. I was. He was relieved I wasn't hurt. Then came the moment I was worried about. He gave me a stern lecture and said that it was going to cost a lot of money to get the radiator fixed, not to mention the tractor was out of commission, and we really needed to get the field ready to plant.

That was the only tractor left that could pull the disc. He was not a happy camper, and I did not blame him in the least. It was all my fault because I thought I was better than I was. I went into the house, where my mother was watching the scene play out from the door. She never said a word, but she certainly kept me busy helping her. I was trusted to get back on the tractor after it was repaired, and I did a decent job from then on. Lesson learned. I continued to drive the trucks and tractors as long as I didn't have to shift gears.

When I was a sophomore in high school, I took the driver's training course for one semester. Apart from a few rules in the handbook that I didn't know about, I was confident this class was going to be a breeze. Finally, the day came when we got to drive the car! This was going to be a blast, and I even got school credit! It's a win/win! I got an A+ in the book part of the course, so I should ace the driving portion, too!

Our driver's training instructor was a nervous little man. He was always tapping his pencil against the window as he rode shotgun in the car. Fortunately, it had a brake on his side, and he used it. It came time to be assigned driving partners. There would be three students and himself in the car, and we would take turns. When he called out the names of the girls I was going to ride with, I secretly cringed. It wasn't that I didn't like them. In fact, the one girl was one of my very best friends. It was just that they were city girls and never, ever sat behind the wheel of a vehicle. Oh, my goodness! The pencil tapping hit an all-time high! The one girl did not curve when the road curved, and she was then driving on the wrong side of the road, with traffic coming the other way! There was some shouting going on in the front seat! I just braced myself for impact. Thankfully, the instructor grabbed the wheel and whipped us over just in time.

The other girl, who was my good friend, was not any better, and to this day, she cannot drive worth a plug nickel. How they ever issued her a license is beyond me. I'm not being mean. She says the same thing! One of our driving days, he needed us to learn how to park. She was up to bat.

He had her take us to the post office and pull into a parking space; then he had us back out. Easy-peasy, right? She pulled into the parking space like a pro. I was proud of her! The instructor said to now back out of the space. She checked all her mirrors, physically turned her head, making sure no one was behind her, and put the car in gear. She turned to look behind her again, gave it too much gas, and we went shooting up and over the sidewalk and right into the post office wall! She had put the car in drive instead of reverse! I was wishing by then that I had a pencil to tap! That took up two full periods at school, getting all the damage accessed and the school, police, and insurance called. Back then, there were no cell phones, so the instructor had to go into the post office and ask to use their phone on top of all the other humiliation. I was happy because I was missing Algebra class! Thank goodness I was sick the day they learned how to parallel park. I taught myself that.

Now came the time to go on the interstate. He had me drive first, so I drove for a while on the interstate—no big deal. I even passed a couple of cars that were going too slow, to which I got "the look," but he still let me do it again. Next up was the "curve" girl. I pulled off to the side of the interstate, and we changed places. She didn't look before she pulled out, and instead of merging back into the lane, she whipped it left and almost smashed into a car going around us. That got us a horn honking, plus a few hand gestures. I wanted to hide. We were running out of time for this session, so the instructor told her we needed to exit the interstate and head back to school. My friend would have to wait and drive up here at the next session.

I said a little prayer of thanksgiving. But while I was doing that, the crazy girl driving took the wrong exit, and instead of continuing up the ramp and going around, she slammed it into reverse, and now we are backing down on the ramp! The instructor blacked out for a few seconds, or else he just froze up. Finally, he got his wits about him and told her to pull over and let someone else drive us back to the school. It should have been my friend's turn, but he turned around in his seat, looked me dead in the eye, and said, "You drive!" I think he picked me not because I was a better driver but because he knew we would get there faster!

Now I'm a junior, and it is time for the prom. The junior class oversaw hosting the prom, so they had to pick a theme and decorate the gym. It was "To Rome with Love!" We blew up hundreds of gold balloons and hung them in clusters to look like grapes; there were several Greek-looking pillars and even a three-tiered water fountain without the water. Classy! All I know is that our apple trees were hanging full of blooms, and Mother said I could cut some branches for the rest of the decorations. What a fabulous idea that was. Not only would it look pretty, but it would also smell wonderful too!

The class worked all day on Thursday, Thursday evening, and most of Friday, putting up these elaborate decorations, but the apple tree branches had to be the very last thing we did so they wouldn't look yucky on Saturday night. We were planning to put them down in big Greek urns of water, but I was not sure how long the blossoms would stay nice, so we knew we had to do it as the last thing on Friday night. I asked my dad if I could borrow the pickup truck to haul the branches in. He said I could, but I needed to get the truck back as soon as I could because it was planting season again, and he might need to use it.

I got the branches delivered and put into place, and one of my good friends asked if I could drop her off at her house on the way home. No problem. As I was heading down the highway, we were talking about her date for the prom, which I had made happen, and she said she'd love to go to the town he was from and maybe we would see him! In my teenage girl's mind, that sounded like a clever idea! But first I had to pass my house to get to the town. Heck, what were the odds of them seeing me drive past? They're still working in the field. I drove past my house, and when I came to the next county road, there sat my dad, waiting to turn onto the highway with the tractor and planter. They must have been working at the other farm!

"I'm dead meat," I told her. But still using my teenage girl's brain, I decided the damage was done, and I might as well keep going. I should have considered spotting Dad as an omen and turned around. The closer I got to town, the guiltier I was becoming. Still, I kept going. We got into town, and I came to a red light. I was going to go straight, but at the last minute, I decided that I should turn right instead. Naturally, I was in the wrong lane to do that. I looked in my mirrors, and no one was in that right lane, I thought, so I turned. My friend just sat there, not saying a word but pointing to her right. I didn't see her point. I was busy driving!

Suddenly, I heard the most awful crunch. I figured out later that she was pointing at a brand-new Cadillac, with the sticker price still on it, that was sitting in that lane. I had turned right into the Cadillac and wedged the truck fender underneath the metal over his front left tire! All that flashed through my mind was a stupid, silly movie where something similar happened, and the guy jumped on the hood of the truck and started jumping up and down, trying to break the vehicles apart. It worked for the guy in the movie, so it will work for me. So, there I am, standing on the hood of the truck, jumping up and down, in the intersection of two main roads in town. It was Friday night, and all the kids were out, running up and down the strip.

I got a lot of horn honks, shouts, and laughter. Finally, the gentleman who had just purchased that brand-new Cadillac got out of his car and came walking up to me, where I was still using the hood as a trampoline. He very softly told me to get down before I got hurt. My eyes began to drop tears down my cheeks. I apologized repeatedly. He saw the tears and told me I had nothing to worry about. No one got hurt, and accidents happened. He was so very kind and treated me so sweetly. I wondered why he was being such a gentleman about it.

Then I saw four girls, slightly younger than me, sitting in the car, laughing their heads off. It turned out he was taking his daughter and some friends to Burger Chef (There's a Blast from the Past!) I guess he wanted to set a good example for the girls to see because no one could be that nice after they get their brand-new Cadillac crunched! Finally, the police arrived, got all the information, and between three strong men, they were able to unhook my bumper from his car. I drove home like a whipped pup. I knew I was in trouble big time. Why didn't I listen to that little voice inside me that said, "Don't go there"? I took my friend to her house, and then I went home to face the music.

By now, Dad had quit for the night, and he was sitting in the kitchen with Mother. Gulp. My mouth was dry, and I could barely get the words out, but I told them what happened. Dad sat there and shook his head back and forth with a frown on his face. But Mother! Oh man, was she furious! She told me I was grounded for two weeks and would not attend the prom the following evening! "But I have my dress and everything!"

"You can wear it next year." For once in my life, I did not argue back with her but just stared at the floor. I deserved everything that I got. I started walking to my room, and Dad said to wait a minute. Oh no, not him, too, I thought. Instead, I got a small sermon about what I did, and then he looked at

Mother and said, "Don't you think she can start her grounding on Sunday and let her go to the prom?"

She looked at him for a long time, then said, "Okay. If that's what you think. However, she is going with me tomorrow morning to the insurance office and will tell Joe exactly what she did! (Joe was a good friend of theirs and also their insurance agent). I did that, and I took the grounding like a champion. I had a wonderful time at the prom, and Dad never said a word about me driving right past him as he sat in his tractor. Maybe he saw me, maybe he did not. He never brought it up, and I sure wasn't going to. I think he saw me, but he just kept quiet because he didn't want to make Mother angrier at me than she already was.

After I graduated from high school, I got married and became the infamous Farmer's Wife. One day, during harvest, Ted's dad was helping with our crops, but they were still short of help. That's when Ted came into the house, asking if I would mind hauling a load or two of corn to the mill. I figured I would pull a wagon with the tractor if he put it in the right gear, and I didn't have to back it up. I'm not good at backing up when I am pulling something. I always manage to jack-knife whatever is behind me. A load of corn would not be good because I could tip that wagon over! Not to worry! He said I had to drive the big grain truck!

"Don't I have to shift gears in that thing?"

"Yeah, but you'll do okay." The problem was not just shifting gears; it was going to be town driving since the mill was on the other side of town. He gave me a quick lesson in gear shifting. A very quick lesson. I hopped in the truck, and the first thing I had to do was pull the seat as far forward as it would go. And I still ended up sitting on the edge of the seat so I could work the clutch, brake, and accelerator. I did not have any problems with the brake or gas pedal. It was that clutch that scared me! I drove very slowly and got to the edge of town with minimal problems until I came to the first stop sign. It was a four-way stop, and a car was already there, so I had to downshift and stop. Hey! I did it! The other car went through; now it was my turn. I already had it in first gear, so all I had to do was let off the clutch and brake and JERK, JERK, JERK all the way through the intersection.

That did not go as well as planned. After doing that a couple more times, I realized I was letting up on the pedals too fast. When the next stop came, I did much better. I was also relieved that no one was behind me. I came to the main street that ran through town and prayed that the stoplights would be green. Not so lucky. The very first stoplight I came to had just turned red. Dang it! It was on a hill! I stopped okay, but cars were coming up and stopping behind me. When the light turned green, I stepped on the clutch, let off the brake slowly, and started rolling backwards! I was almost on top of the car behind me! I panicked and stomped on the brake. My mind went completely blank! What am I supposed to do? I was scared to death that I would roll right on top of the hood of that car!

People behind me were aggravated because I wasn't going forward, and I am sure the driver in the car behind me was making out their will. I took a deep breath, and with my foot on the clutch and brake, I made sure it was in first gear and let out on the clutch and brake very slowly. I was going forward! It didn't even jerk that bad. (It jerked a little because some corn splattered on top of the car behind me.) but I was still going forward. I had to repeat this action for four other stoplights until I reached the mill. I managed without too much trouble. As the grain was being dumped into the pit at the mill, I glanced at the rearview mirror. Yep! I had a few more grey hairs, courtesy of Ted, and I was only in my twenties. What am I going to look like in my forties if I stay married to him? However, I would have missed all those surprises he sprung on me throughout our marriage. Plus, I did learn how to drive a clutch!

We both worked for my dad's grain handling company, which was right across the road from where we lived. We sold grain bins, grain dryers, heaters and fans, transport augers, and the parts that went with them. Ted was the sales and service manager, and I was the lowly receptionist/secretary/go-for/and janitor. Ted also trained me to get parts, and I was actually pretty good at it if it was something simple. Ninety-nine percent of our customers were men, with the occasional wife thrown in on a parts run. At first, I had a tough time showing the men that I could help them despite being a woman. I finally won them over, and it got so that they trusted me, only if Ted weren't there to help them.

Whether he wanted it or not, Ted had found his niche in life. Everybody loved dealing with him because he knew what he was doing, and he was not out to rob them by just selling new parts. He genuinely cared about his customers and tried to save them as much money as he could. If something could be fixed, he fixed it instead of making them buy a new one. It wasn't the right thing to do to make the company lots of money, but it was surely the most ethical and decent thing to do, and our customers knew that. To this day, he still is in the grain handling business, and his old customers, customers' sons, and sometimes, even the customers' grandsons still rely on Ted to give them the correct advice. His reputation grew, and he is now well known throughout the Tri-state area. Maybe even farther. He was selling equipment far and wide.

One day, Mother came over to the office. She was upset because her aunt had just passed away. Mother was from the northern part of the state, where she grew up very close to her family. So, this aunt's death really upset her. The visitation was on a Friday evening, with the funeral on

Saturday. She wanted to let me know that they would be gone, and I was in charge of getting in the mail and all the other little jobs I had when she left. Okay. No problem. Or so I thought!

Ted overheard our conversation, and when she left, he came up to my desk and said how sorry he was to hear of my great-aunt's passing. "Thanks, but I barely knew her."

"Still, she is your mom's aunt, and I could tell she was pretty upset. I think you should plan to go to the visitation also."

"Not necessary," I said, but he insisted I go, just to support Mother. He finally convinced me to go.

The next day was Thursday, and he came up to my desk and said, "I just thought of something! I sold a transport auger awfully close to the town you will be going to. I have been trying to figure out a way to get it up there. How about you leave early and drop it off on your way to the visitation?" AH-HA! He did not give a hoot about me supporting my mother in her hour of need. He needed to get that auger up to the farmer and saw a terrific opportunity to kill two birds with one stone.

The only trouble is, I had never pulled a transport auger in my life! For everyone who doesn't know, a transport auger is a piece of equipment for getting your grain into the storage bin. They come in many sizes, up to 110 feet long or more and up to 13" in diameter. It is a long, round metal tube that has a huge corkscrew-looking thing inside, and when you turn it on and dump your grain in the bottom, it takes the grain all the way to the top of the bin and drops it through a hole in the roof. This tube is fixed on a steel frame on wheels so it can be pulled from bin to bin and farm to farm. The makers try to keep them sized so they can be pulled down the road if necessary.

The part about me never pulling one in my life did not faze him. He said he would get it hooked up to the truck (automatic, thank goodness!), and I could practice driving it around the buildings. I told him the only way I knew how to get there was down the interstate. Is this thing legal on the interstate? He never really answered my question. He just told me to keep the flashers on, stay in the right-hand lane, and if I got pulled over, play dumb. I got the "playing dumb" part down. I have had lots of practice with that. I gave out a big sigh and agreed to do it.

Friday morning came, and my chariot awaited. It was all gassed up, hooked up, and ready to go, with a big red flag hanging from the back so traffic could see me from behind. The last thing I needed was a semi running into the top and slamming it into his windshield! As I climbed in the truck, he gave me one more piece of advice: "Be sure to swing wide when you're turning and watch out for overhead wires." That got me thinking about the overpasses I would be going under. I mentioned that to him, and he said a bit hesitatingly,

"Oh, you will be fine. Just be sure to slow down a little so if you hit a bump, it doesn't bounce up and whack the end of the auger." Oh great. Now I have something else to worry about. Is there any question about why I have ulcers?

Off I went, headed to town without incident. I swung wide at the corners and watched for overhead wires. I made it to the interstate and merged into traffic like a pro. The traffic was kind. They gave me plenty of room and were not impatient with me for driving slower. I went along my merry way, patting myself on the back, when I checked the clock. In my tiny brain, I calculated that I would be getting on the major six-lane bypass around our state's capital city about rush hour on a Friday night! My heart started racing, and I started getting nauseous, but I could not do anything except keep going and praying. I tried merging onto the bypass, but it was bumper-to-bumper traffic, and they sure were not going to get over for me. They were all on a mission to get home for the weekend. Finally, a kind semi flashed his lights, and I took it as a sign to pull out, which I did. I stayed in the right-hand lane while frustrated drivers were racing past me. I did this for about forty-five minutes until it was time to exit off and continue North for another hour. After going to the wrong farm first, I finally found the right place and pulled in. I waited for someone to come out and get this thing unhooked for me. I waited and waited, but no one ever came.

I climbed out of the truck and did it myself at the hitch. When the guys at the office hooked the auger up, Ted must have told them to be sure to secure it tight. He didn't want it coming unhooked while I was driving. It happened before, not to me, but to somebody else, so he was being cautious. They had it chained with a log chain and wrapped so tight I could not budge it. I looked for some tools but came up empty. I finally found a rock and smacked the chain with the rock. It seemed to help, for whatever reason, so I continued to smack it until it was loose enough so I could unwrap the chain. I pulled the hitch pin and drove off, headed towards the funeral home. After all, that was the real reason I was here, wasn't it?

I walked into the funeral home and was greeted by lots of cousins, aunts, and uncles. They were all happy to see me, and we talked and talked. I was there for about an hour before I spotted Dad sitting alone on a couch. He looked at me very strangely but never said anything. I told him I had delivered an auger, and he seemed shocked that I did, but he said, "That explains it."

"What?"

"You'd better go look in the mirror. I found the bathroom, looked in the mirror, and scared myself! I had dirt and grease smeared all over my face and clothes. I must have gotten it from the chain and did not notice. My hands were black, my face and clothes had huge grease smears, and they were all topped off with rock dust from hitting it so hard on the chain. I looked like a mechanic who spent his day underneath a car. I was so mortified I could have cried. All those relatives, whom I had not seen in such a long time, probably thought I lived in the dumpster in an alley somewhere! I was so angry, but who could I be angry at? Ted had the guys secure it tight for my own safety. He didn't know the chain was covered with grease. He also didn't know the farmer would not be there to unhook it himself.

After cleaning up the best I could, I said my goodbyes and headed home. By the time I got there, I was too tired to gripe at anyone. As I walked upstairs, Ted said, "What's all that black stuff on the back of your legs?" Really?

As I said before, Ted had a reputation for being the "Answer Man," as I called him, about anything pertaining to grain handling. So much so that a global company that we dealt with offered him a job running a new warehouse, they were going to open. It would take care of all the dealers on this side of the Mississippi. He took the job, and I went with him. His customers followed him there, even though it was two and a half hours farther north than where we used to work. They continued to buy equipment, and when they bought a transport auger, I had the privilege of delivering it to them. The first few trips were nail-biters, but I got surprisingly good at it after a while.

I only had one little goof in that entire time. A fast-food restaurant on a corner where I always turned decided to put a huge boulder at the corner in their property. I wasn't used to that being there, and I turned like I always did. Only this time, the wheel of the auger went up, and over that huge boulder, and for a split second, the auger was almost sideways going around the corner! I thought for sure it was going to tip all the way over on the oncoming traffic, but as quickly as I could blink, it fell back to the street and leveled itself out. I dodged a bullet on that one!

I continued to be the auger delivery person for about seven years until Ted and I decided we wanted to go back home. The only thing that I could have done better was learn to back those things up. I tried a couple of times and ended up jack-knifed every time. I would drive two to three hours pulling one down the road, I would get it to the customer's farm, and the guy would come out and say, "Just put it over there."

At that time, I would hop out of the truck and say, "Nope! I can only go forward! You'll have to back it up yourself!"

You can't fight city hall, or can you?

The summer between second and third grade, my best friend and I got ourselves in a heap of trouble. It all started when the school board decided they needed to change all the school districts in the county. No one knows why. If it ain't broke, don't fix it! What a mess!

I lived on the edge of all the school districts. I had four different school buses going to four different schools that drove past my house each day. My best friend at the time lived a mile down the county road next to my house, and she had three different buses for three different schools drive past hers. I went to a school north of us, and she went to a school south of us. I guess they had to draw the line somewhere, but our entire community was torn up.

There were a few people on the board who decided to make themselves look busy, so they drew up a map of the county and decided a bunch of us needed to be shipped off to a different school. The school I was going to at the time was seven miles away. The school my friend went to was about ten miles away. The third school was farther north, and it was about eleven miles away. But the school these "wise ones" wanted to send all of us to was over twenty miles away!

My mother and my friend's mom were really upset because that would mean I would have to get on the bus at about 6:30 in the morning and not get home until 5:30 in the evening. That was nuts! The women contacted all the other parents who were going to be included in this stupid move, and it did not take long until they became a force to deal with! They tried to talk to the board in a civilized manner, but the president of the board was on a power trip. I think he had "Little Man Syndrome" like Napoleon Bonaparte had. He just expected everyone to do what he said. He would not even negotiate. After our group tried to play nice, and it did not work, the parents hired a lawyer. Maybe "Napoleon" would talk to him. I must say, this little guy had a lot of nerve because he refused to talk to the lawyer and said we would lose the case if we sued the board. When the parents considered that a threat, a lawsuit was drawn up.

When the rest of the school board heard about the lawsuit, they wanted to talk to the parents and hear what they had to say. It had only been one guy talking until now. He did things behind the school board's back that they later found out were unethical and went against the board's policies. They called a special meeting once the rest of the board heard what he had done.

Apparently, "Napoleon" threatened any school board member who was going to go against him. Some buckled under his pressure, and others stood up for us. They took a vote, and it was decided a meeting would be held so they could hear the parents' arguments. "Napoleon" set it for midday, when most of the parents were working, which is what he was planning on. The parents were all up in arms, and their lawyer stepped in and made the board schedule the meeting for an evening at the courthouse so everyone could attend the meeting and be heard.

This is where my better judgment came into question. My friend and I were too young to stay home alone, and everyone we could stay with was attending the meeting. My parents and her parents decided we would all ride together in one car, and they would let my friend and I sit in the car with the doors locked until the meeting was over. So many people showed up for the meeting that we could not find a place to park, and we ended up parking down a side street.

Our moms had bought us all kinds of stuff to keep us entertained while they were slaying the dragon at the courthouse. We had coloring books and new crayons, puzzle books, games, and lots and lots of snacks. When the grown-ups got out of the car, they told us again to keep the doors locked, and we had better not set foot outside that car, or else!

We colored and ate snacks. We played games and ate snacks. We did puzzles and ate snacks. We talked, and the entire time we ate snacks. Do you notice I said we ate snacks, but we did not drink anything? Eating all those salty snacks made our throat and lips feel parched. I'm not sure who said it first, but we both decided that we needed a drink or we would surely die. We scrounged around, found a couple of dimes under the seat, and found more change in the ashtray. Times were different back then, and cars came standard with cigarette lighters and ashtrays in the front and back seats. The change we found was in the back ashtray, so it probably belonged to my friend's big brother, so we figured it was fair game. He reminded me of Eddie Haskell on Leave It to Beaver.

We counted the money, and we had more than enough to get us a soda. My friend said she thought she knew where the gas station was, and they had a Coke machine. I had no idea where I was, so I just followed her lead. We got out of the car, being careful not to lock it because we did not have the keys. We started walking. Surely, one of these streets would take us to a gas station. We walked and walked until we saw a Shell sign high in the air.

"There it is! I told you I knew where it was!" We found the Coke machine, put the money in, and plop, a can fell out. We only found enough money for one can, so we had to share it. She took a drink, I took a drink, back and forth like that until it was empty. We had to drink it there so we could pitch the evidence in the trash. We felt much better!

Now we'd better get back to the car before our parents come out of the meeting and catch us!

I looked at her and asked, "Which way do we need to go?"

"I think we need to walk this way." So off we went. Only that was the wrong way. Nothing looked familiar at all! I did not remember passing any of these houses on the way. "Oh, we probably just need to go over one street." We did, and it was wrong, too. We were lost, but neither one of us wanted to say it. We wandered around for what seemed like hours. It was dark by now, and that made things hard to see and very scary to a couple of six-year-old girls. I wanted to cry. We had been going in the completely opposite direction from the car, we later figured out. Once we got headed in the right direction, we finally spotted the car and ran like the boogie man was after us. Thank goodness our parents were not back yet! We both would have been killed right on the spot. We jumped into the back seat and locked the doors.

We finally caught our breath, and our hearts quit beating a mile a minute. We settled back and started playing another game, but it was too dark in the car to see particularly good. We sat and talked awhile; then I remembered a ball I found under their back seat when I was looking for the money. I bent down and got it, and pitched it to my friend. She pitched it back. We did that for a short time until she unlocked the door next to the sidewalk and climbed out. I sat on the seat, half in and half out. We pitched the ball back and forth, and we could see fairly well with the streetlight.

We were so engrossed in our little game of pitch and catch that we did not see four adult figures round the corner and start walking towards us. Oh no! It's our parents! She jumped back in the car and locked the door. The jig was up! They saw us. Goodbye, my friend. It was great knowing you all these years. We are going to get killed now.

Needless to say, we were yelled at all the way home. They dropped us off at our house, and I slowly walked in. My mother was still ranting at me when I got in the house. She finally stopped yelling and told me to go downstairs and get a ping-pong paddle. That was to be her weapon of punishment. Well played, Mother! She had me bend over her knee, she raised the paddle in the air, and just like the governor stopping execution in prison, my dad spoke up and said, "Just let her go this time. She learned her lesson." I ran over, hugged him, and told him I was so sorry. Then, I did what any other six-year-old would have done.

I said, "It was all her idea!"

Several years later, when my friend and I were both seniors in high school, her English Literature teacher gave the class an assignment. They were to write about an adventure that they experienced. She chose to write about that fateful night when we walked all over the south end of town, looking for our car. Her dad happened to be a teacher at the school, and he got wind of the assignment and the paper she wrote. Can you believe her parents grounded her for three weeks? Shouldn't the statute of limitations be honored? Heavens! That was over ten years ago! I guess I did not have the strictest parents on the planet after all!

A faithful friend for life!

When the company we worked for started to grow, we knew we needed to make some changes. Ted had grown quite a customer following, and they came to him for everything. We decided we needed a parts department and showroom. When it was almost completed, we had to decide what was going on in it and how we were going to display it.

We heard that the Five and Dime store in town was going out of business, and they were selling everything from wall to wall. Ted thought that would be the perfect opportunity to get the shelving and display cases for our parts department. When the day of the sale came, we went there bright and early to make sure we bought everything we needed. We made out like bandits! We had a full trailer load of shelves and cabinets, and there was still more stuff for a second load. While we waited for the empty trailer to return, the owner said we were welcome to go upstairs and see if there was anything we would like to buy.

The upstairs was used for storage, and it was musty and dingy, but we did see a couple of desks that we purchased. I ventured down the dark hallway, and there was a door that was only half open. When I pushed the door open, I got the fright of my life! The room was dark, but I could tell it was full of naked people, all intertwined! What the heck are they doing in there? Then I realized that they were not moving.

They were mannequins the store used to display the new fashions they sold! I giggled to myself about how crazy they all looked.

After we looked at the rest of the furniture, we decided we had enough to accomplish what we wanted. Then I started thinking. I would love to have one of those mannequins! I asked Ted if I could buy one. "What on earth for?"

"I can use it for lots of things!"

"Name one," he said.

"Well, I'm not sure just now, but I know I will use it for stuff. Please?" So, he asked the owner how much he wanted for the mannequins. He told Ted that most of them were already sold. He just had one mannequin left, and it was a man.

"I'll take it!" So, we went back upstairs to collect our man!

There he stood, surrounded by all the women mannequins. Poor fella. I bet he is going to hate leaving this place. As I got closer to him, I noticed a few odd things about him. Someone had used a brown marker and drew a beard on him, I guess to make him look more manly. He probably was the model for the flannel shirts and work jeans. I bet he looked just like a lumberjack. Then I noticed his hands. Oh, my goodness! They were women's hands! And the fingernails were long, pointed, and polished, a pretty shade of bright pink!

"What in the world is up with his hands?" The owner said that his hands had a slight accident, so they had to borrow a pair of hands from one of the women's mannequins.

"The nice thing about all these guys is that their parts are interchangeable."

"Do you have any man hands?" I asked.

"No, his hands lost all his fingers in a bizarre elevator accident, and I am afraid all we have are lady's hands. People won't notice his hands." Oh, I definitely think people will notice a rugged man with long, slender fingers and bright pink nail polish!

We loaded him up and took him to his new home. Then I noticed another thing about this guy. Not only did he have lady hands, but both were left hands! He did not even have a right hand! I put a pair of Ted's old jeans and a shirt on him. Then I found a pair of Ted's old work shoes and struggled to get him into those. I stood back and looked at him. He looked just like he was ready to hop on a tractor or build a grain bin. Then A light bulb went off! I will put him in the parts department and use him for advertising! It will be so much fun to produce different scenarios for him. The customers will love it! I told Ted what I wanted to do, and he didn't seem to care one way or another, so I took the idea and ran with it!

It was Saturday morning, and I decided to take the mannequin over to the parts department and stake out a spot where I could put him. The poor guy could not bend, so I opened the car's back door and started sliding him in on the seat sideways like he was lying down. My son happened to wake up, looked out the window, and saw two jean-covered legs sticking stiffly out of the car with Ted's old work shoes on.

He quickly opened his window and yelled, "What are you doing to Dad? Is he okay?" I had to pull the guy back out of the car so my son could see that it wasn't his dad.

I needed to give the mannequin a name. Ted and my dad were always teasing each other and joking around. Dad always called Ted "Fred," after Sanford and Son, the TV show where the father (Fred) and his son (Lamont) ran a junkyard. Fred was always wheelin' and dealin' just like Ted did. Ted would take the oldest, most run-down piece of equipment on trade, fix it up so it would run, and find a buyer for it, just like old Fred did. I decided the only appropriate name for the mannequin would be Lamont! When Dad came through the door, he laughed, and I introduced him to Lamont. He got a big chuckle out of that! When the lights were out at nighttime, all you could see was a silhouette of a man standing in the darkroom by the door. It was creepy at first, but soon, he became just one of the guys that worked with us.

Over the next couple of years, I had fun displaying different scenarios that matched the season and tied it into our company. He was a Pilgrim for Thanksgiving, with Lamont dressed all in black, sporting a Pilgrim hat and a sign that said, "We are thankful for all our farmers during the Holiday season." Of course, I always had to keep gloves on him to cover up his two feminine hands! At Halloween one year, I wrapped him up tight in gauze so he looked like a mummy and smudged black powder on him and his face in different spots. I stuck a crazy wig on him and gelled the hair so it stuck straight out in all directions. He looked like he had stuck his finger in a light socket. "Having electrical problems with your equipment? Don't try to fix it yourself, or you could end up just like Lamont! Let our trained service techs help!" I got a lot of reactions to that one. He was Santa for Christmas, of course, and Cupid for Valentine's Day. He was Uncle Sam in July and wore swim trunks in August, all with clever signs that would bring attention to whatever we were promoting at the time.

When my dad decided it was time to retire, he turned the business over to the manager full-time, and he walked away. That was a sad day. Not only did he leave, but so did all the fun and happiness we had working there. Once Dad was gone, the manager felt we needed to stop joking around and be serious. He also told me to get Lamont out of the parts department. It broke my heart, and after I took him away, several customers asked us where Lamont went. I told them, point blank, that the fuddy-duddy in charge told me to get rid of him. "That is a shame. I always enjoyed seeing what Lamont was up to when I came in!"

I was not going to just let Lamont stand in our garage without a purpose in life. I could at least give him a life at Halloween and Christmas! When trick-or-treat time came, I dressed him up like Frankenstein and stood him on the front porch with a spotlight shining on him. I thought it looked cool, but a few of the youngest trick-or-treaters did not want to come to the door with Lamont standing there!

Christmastime came, and Lamont was going to be Santa again. I stood next to the front door, this time like he was getting ready to come inside. I even had a big red bag full of wrapped boxes sitting behind him. He was doing an excellent job, making our house look so festive, until one night, a strong gust of wind blew through and blew him over. He fell down on our concrete porch, so when anyone drove past during the night, the spotlight was shown on what looked like a drunken Santa that had passed out! Unfortunately, his face, which was made of that old plaster, took a beating. His face was cracked, and his nose got pushed back into his head. I wanted to cry! I took him into the house and was able to pull his nose back out with some tweezers. Then I rubbed clear glue all over his face and let it dry. It seemed to have done the trick! At least it would keep all the little bits of plaster in place and not crumble to the ground. I stuck his white beard back on, and you could not even tell he had had an accident!

I learned my lesson, though. I put him back by the front door again, but this time, I stood him under the porch light, ran a thin wire under his beard and around his neck, and securely wired it to the porch light! That should prevent him from falling over. I patted myself on the back because I was so clever.

The next morning, the wind was still very gusty, but I could see part of Lamont's red suit from the side window, and I knew he was still standing. When it was time for the kids to get on the school bus, I opened the door and was met by a scene out of one of those poorly made horror movies! Yes, Lamont was still in an upright position. However, the wind had taken his feet out from under him, and he was just hanging by his neck like a bad guy in a Western movie! It literally looked like I lynched him! Plus, the spotlight was still shining on the horrible scene! Everybody that went to work that morning probably thought I needed therapy. "How could she hang Santa for all the little kids to see?" I know I traumatized several little kids on the school bus that morning.

Now, it was time to bring in the "Answer Man." He thought about what we could do and got the problem fixed. He weighed Lamont's feet down with heavy rocks, then placed the big red bag full of gifts in front of him so it hid his feet. Lamont stood guard for the rest of the Christmas season. Then, it was time to give him a well-deserved rest in our garage. I stood Lamont in the corner, out of the way, until the next time his services were needed. Unfortunately, our cats got into a huge fight and knocked him over, this time crushing his face completely. There on the concrete floor lay his nose and lips. His forehead was smashed in, and one ear was dangling. His chin was in a million little pieces. There was no way he could be fixed. I really did cry this time.

I could not bring myself to do anything with him. He had become part of the family! We put him on life support, but we knew we really needed just to pull the plug. Poor Lamont. What are we going to do without you?

Ted and I talked, and we both decided we could not throw him in the garbage can. The guys picking up our trash would call the sheriff on us for trying to dispose of a body! Even if it was short-lived, we did not need to make the newspaper's front page. We decided to wait until a perfect opportunity came along to send him to his final resting place. He went back into the garage corner, only we laid him down, giving him the dignity he deserved.

I finally got through the mourning process, and after a while, life went on. Then, one warm spring day, I caught Ted at the perfect moment, and he agreed to help me clean out the garage. I don't know why, but in the summer, when we are in and out all the time, the garage stays tidy, but in the wintertime, we toss stuff everywhere just to get back inside the warm house. We were looking at a full day of cleaning and pitching.

We made several piles. Stuff to keep and put away, stuff that could be recycled, junk that just needed to be thrown in the dumpster, and one pile for anything burnable. Since Ted was the official fire starter, I let him oversee the burnables. The more we accumulated, the happier he got! We finally finished; everything was put in its place, the recyclables were loaded in the back of Ted's truck to take away, and the burnable stuff was carried back to our infamous burn pile. There was nothing left to do except address Lamont.

We had a big pile of stuff that could be burned, so Ted went back to the burn pile, armed with a lighter and a water hose, just in case. He set fire to some papers, and off it went. After the fire settled down, he came back and asked me what we should do with Lamont. Finally, he and I agreed that Lamont needed to be cremated. Ted picked him up and carried him upside down across the yard. I am sure he got some strange looks from passersby, wondering what that man was doing carrying the other man like that. Lamont did not have a shirt or shoes on, but he did still have on his pair of old jeans. One car even honked, but we have learned to ignore the honking over the years since we do so many things that deserve a good toot.

Once Ted got to the burning pile of stuff, he tossed Lamont in, and he somehow landed on his head, with his feet and jean-covered legs sticking straight up in the air. If I had a trumpet, I would have played "Taps." However, it just does not have the same effect playing it on my saxophone.

Ever so slowly, Lamont started to melt—first his crushed face, then his shoulders, chest, and arms. I am not sure how he remained sticking straight up. I think it was Lamont's final gesture of being a faithful friend. As he continued to melt, he reminded me of the Wicked Witch in the movie The Wizard of Oz. after she got splashed with a bucket of water. "I'm melting, I'm melting! Oh, what a world, what a world!" And then he was gone.

I imagine everyone driving past had a crazy story to tell when they got to their destination, seeing us burning a man alive! I'm shocked that we didn't get paid a visit from law enforcement. But I suppose, when someone tried to tell the sheriff what we were doing, he just shrugged and said, "It's just the Hahns, being the Hahns. It's normal." Really?